THE MANY WORLDS OF SCIENCE FICTION

THE MANY WORLDS OF SCIENCE FICTION

edited by BEN BOVA

E. P. DUTTON & CO., INC. NEW YORK

To John W. Campbell

"All Cats Are Gray," by Andre Norton, appeared in *Fantastic Universe* magazine (1953).

Published simultaneously in Canada by Clarke, Irwin & Company Limited, Toronto and Vancouver

SBN: 0-525-34550-7 LCC: 75-162276

Designed by Hilda Scott
Printed in the U.S.A.
First Edition

CONTENTS

THE MANY WORLDS OF SCIENCE FICTION

Introduction

The purpose of this book is to show "where it's at" in the science fiction world today. For science fiction is a broad, exciting field that encompasses a rich variety of subject matter, writing styles, and personal attitudes. That's what we mean by "the many worlds" of science fiction.

In fact, this book should really be titled "The Many Worlds of SF." For nowadays the term SF is often used instead of "science fiction." Depending on who's doing the talking, SF can mean science fiction, science fantasy, speculative fiction, or even scientific fantabulation (which sounds almost as grotesque as the quaint old term, sci fi). In short, SF goes far beyond the heavily technological space operas of yesteryear.

Science fiction has often been unfairly downgraded as pulp literature, usually by people who never took the trouble to look past the garish cover of a science fiction magazine. But even in the most heavily technical, off-to-Mars, shoot-the-monster stories, science fiction offered something to its readers that attracted and held them. Some people called this attraction "a sense of wonder." Others pointed out that science fiction is a literature of ideas, a literature of change, and in a world where change is dizzyingly apparent, science fiction speaks directly about the real world around us.

by BEN BOVA

Today, the many worlds of SF include many stories that have nary a spaceship nor a robot in them: stories that take place here and now, as well as millennia in the future; stories that use elements of fantasy as well as technology; stories that are lush with exotic backgrounds and strong with provocative ideas; stories that make you think.

Take a look at the stories in this book. Several of them deal with war. Others are about the integrity of the individual in a complex society. All of them examine the worth of a human being when pitted against an uncaring or even hostile universe.

And look at the many different ways these themes are handled. Both Gene Wolfe's and Burt Filer's stories are about war, but no two stories could be farther apart in treatment or style. Yet each says something significant about the human spirit in the face of war.

Andre Norton and Anne McCaffrey both present us with female protagonists. Yet there the similarity between the two stories ends. Miss Norton gives us high adventure among the stars. Miss McCaffrey shows the problems of a girl facing the responsibilities of adulthood.

Robert Silverberg, Keith Laumer, and Gordon Dickson each have alien creatures playing central roles in their stories. But there are no bug-eyed monsters among them. These aliens are not only believable, but they serve to contrast and define the human reactions of the Earthmen in these stories.

Harlan Ellison tells a pyrotechnical story about man's responsibility to be true to himself, and he draws his material about equally from today's headlines and from the imaginative treasures of fantasy.

Despite the wild differences of theme and treatment, though, each of these stories is about people. Human beings, like us. For all the many worlds of SF revolve around human emotions and human actions. These stories show many different facets of humanity. They use SF's great freedom of time and place to put their people into situations that test their humanity in special, dramatically striking ways.

One more thing. The stories, at heart, are meant to entertain you. If you do read SF often, I think you'll find them among the best you can get. And if you're new to SF, I certainly hope that these eight tales will serve as a beginning to a long and warm friendship.

Ben Bova

Arlington, Massachusetts
January 1971

The Blue Mouse

INTRODUCTION

War is an atrocity because it makes murder heroic. Gene Wolfe has seen war firsthand, in Korea, and has written a story about what war does to a youth who does not want to fight or kill.

Born in Brooklyn, raised in Houston, Gene Wolfe began reading science fiction pulp magazines while hiding behind the candy case in his neighborhood drugstore. His reading habits eventually expanded, due mainly to school, to include Edgar Allan Poe, Thomas Wolfe (no relation), Ernest Hemingway. He began writing in 1956, shortly after getting married. His stories have appeared in many magazines and in SF collections such as the "Orbit" series, Again Dangerous Visions, *and* Alchemy and Academe. *His first novel,* Operation Ares, *was published in 1970.*

Soft-spoken, thoughtful, and thought-provoking, Gene Wolfe turns out stories that have a distinctive quality. Often they are about teen-aged boys on the verge of manhood. "The Blue Mouse" *is about a youth who faces the true horror of war: kill or be killed.*

by GENE WOLFE

IT'S an awful thing you're doing," the old woman said, "an awful, terrible thing. How old are you, anyway? Have another cookie." Her voice was as thin as the wind that tossed her gray hair against the background of winter-gray hills.

"Eighteen." Lonnie accepted the cookie, with one in his mouth already and another in his throat. They were large, and the sour milk and brown sugar the old woman had used had given them a scratchy and persistent crumb. A big raisin occupied the center of each.

"You're but a little lad and not responsible," the old woman said, "but if you'd seen the half of all I have, you'd not be here killin' our boys."

Lonnie, whose two meters plus towered over her, nodded —knowing she would not listen if he tried to defend the Peace Force. A sip of the warm, weak tea she had given him softened cookies number one and two enough for him to swallow number three.

"And where would you be from?"

He gave her the name of his home city. From her blank expression he knew she had never heard of it. She said, "What country was it, I meant."

The crumbs clung to the front of his blue fatigue shirt, and he tried to brush them off. "Sector ten," he said.

She helped him absently, smoothing the wrinkled twill with age-crooked fingers. "And where is that?"

"South of nine, close to the Great Lakes. If you don't want us here putting down the unrest—" (it was always called "the unrest" in orientation lectures, and he felt an obligation, here alone by the old woman's tumbledown stone cottage, to represent the official view) "—why are you giving me the cookies and tea?"

"It said to do it on the tel. Our free channel. It says we does our part by tellin' you it's wrong that you should come here killin'. And it's easy enough to do—you're nice enough lads, the ones I've talked with." The wind was rising, and she took her free hand, the one not holding the blue-rimmed plate of cookies, away from his shirt to keep her skirt in place.

Lonnie said, "I don't kill anyone. I'm a Tech, not a Marksman."

"It's the same. You're carrying the bullets that will take the lives of boys here."

"It's not ammunition." He glanced toward the road, where his loaded truck stood with its launcher slanted at the sky. "Mostly it's winter clothes."

"It's the same," the old woman said stubbornly. (Up there the wild geese were calling, lost in the gray clouds. There was a feeling of rain.) "Never mind. You but think on it that our lads are only wanting to be free of the foreign law, and the greasy dark foreigners followin' your blue rag half 'round the world to suck our blood. Think on it, if you should find such a thing as a conscience about you."

Later, as Lonnie jolted along in the truck, the rain came. A sensor near the windshield detected it and sprayed out a detergent, transforming the drops into a cleansing film more optically flat and transparent than the polycarbonate windshield itself. Lonnie set the autodriver for MUD and switched it in. Occasionally, the insurgents cut the guide cables or pulled a slack section into a bog, but at such low speed he would be able to regain control if necessary, and he wanted to send a letter. He got out his Hallmark Voisriit.

"Dear Mother," he said. The feedback screen, showing the picture which on his mother's own viewer would accompany his voice, displayed a cartooned soldier ignoring exploding shells; the balloon over his head held the ezspeek words, "*Hii thair,*" and an exclamation point.

"October 15th. Dear Mother. I don't have a great deal to say, but I've some time on my hands right now and I wanted to tell you everything's all right here and really very quiet. It's damp and cold, but our tents are warm and dry. You asked if I still believed in what we're supposed to be doing. Yes I do, but I see it more clearly. It's not only whether or not we're going to let the world slip backward into nationalism and war, but—"

The truck topped a hill and he saw the wet plastic of the battalion tents. He had not realized there was so short a distance yet to go; sighing, he touched the *eeraas* button and slipped the Voisriit back into its leatheroid envelope, then took over from the autodriver.

The road dove between high tangles of wire, and the camp unfolded around him. The battalion supply tents, where he was going, were at the end of the road. Beyond them, linked to the road by a rutted track, lay the tank park with its three hunchbacked hard-shell tanks and the combat cars. The Battalion Headquarters tents and the SAM-guarded helicopter pad flanked the road; and from it the company streets of the four Marksman companies branched at measured intervals, with that of his own Headquarters Company and the motor pool parking area further on.

Surrounding everything was the network of Marksman trenches and strong points, with computer-directed guns and launchers thrust forward to enfilade attackers, raking their advance from the side if they tried to overrun the trenches. Lonnie recalled that when he had first been assigned here he had thought these, with the wire and the mine fields, were impregnable. He had soon been enlightened by more experienced men. Leaving aside the chemical, viral, and nuclear weapons neither side dared use, there remained the ancient arithmetic of men. There were, all in all, blue-uniformed Techs and green-shirted Marksmen, a thousand United Nations soldiers defending this small outpost of the Peace Force. In the hills surrounding it, and in villages where they waited the order to take up arms, were perhaps fifty thousand insurgents.

He had helped the supply staff unload his truck and was about to see if it were still too early to get supper at the mess hall, when one of the supply clerks said casually, "Captain Koppel wants to see you." Koppel was Battalion Intelligence Officer.

"What for?"

"He didn't say. Just to send you over."

Lonnie nodded and put on his poncho, though he was already soaked from unloading without it. Rain slanted into his eyes as he left the tent.

A Marksman in green, matte-finished armor, with weary

eyes like caves, moved cautiously aside for him. Techs, who did not fight, who according to the psychological tests administered at induction, *would not* fight, sometimes had been known to trip or strike a passing Marksman from behind. Marksmen were usually almost too exhausted to protest, and more often than might be expected were physically small. Lonnie himself—once (he told himself)—only once . . .

There had been five of them, friends from camp, full of beer and bravery after completing the "tough" training course. They had surprised two Marksmen on the gravel parking lot of a roadside joint with savage, wide-swung head punches until—

He blinked the image away, turned into the HQ tent, and saluted. "Tech Specialist Third Leonard P. Daws, sir."

"At ease, Daws." Captain Koppel was a blue-uniformed Tech like himself despite his rank, a man heavily forty with an intelligent, unworldly face that seemed designed for a clergyman. "You've just returned from Corps?"

"From Corps supply dump, sir."

"The road was clear?"

"Yes, sir."

"You saw no signs of the enemy?"

"No, sir. Only an old woman."

"Did you converse with her?"

Lonnie paused. "Only for a few minutes, sir. The orientation lectures always say that we're to behave well toward the civilian population and be friendly, so I thought it couldn't do much harm, sir."

The captain nodded. "Who initiated the contact, you or she?"

"I guess she did, sir. She has a cottage on the road about

twenty kilometers up, and when she heard my truck coming she came out with a plate of cookies and some tea, so I stopped."

"I see. Go on."

"Well, that's about all there is to it, sir."

"Oh, come now. You're an intelligent young man, Daws —didn't somebody tell me you had some college?"

"A semester, sir, before I was inducted. Biology."

"Then you should be able to guess the sort of thing I want to know. Did this old lady of yours favor their side or ours? Did she pump you about anything? Did she try to subvert you?"

"Theirs, sir. I wouldn't say she really questioned me, but she more or less said I had ammunition in the truck, and I told her I didn't. Also, she asked what country I was from, and I told her Ten."

The captain pursed his lips. "I don't want you to get the wrong impression of our situation, Daws. It's not at all serious, and there's no question of our ability to maintain the integrity of our perimeter no matter what's thrown at us, but the guide cable has been cut. Did you know that?"

"No, sir. I came in on it for the last five kilometers or so and it seemed okay then."

"It was severed on the far side of the river, just over the bridge—we think. How long have you been in camp?"

"About an hour, sir. I helped unload before I came here."

"You should have come at once."

Lonnie stood a little straighter. The Supply sergeant and his men, he knew, had waited until he had helped unload before passing on Koppel's message. "I didn't think it was urgent, sir," he said.

"We sent out a repair crew and they ambushed them.

Some of them surrendered and they killed them, too, Techs as well as Marksmen. You didn't see anything?"

"No, sir."

"Listen, Daws," the captain stood up, and walking around his desk put a hand on Lonnie's shoulder. "You have a gun mounted on that truck of yours, don't you?"

"An eighteen millimeter launcher, sir. The autodriver controls it once I turn it on. I would have used it if I'd seen anything, sir."

"I hope you would. Let me tell you something, Daws. If we win this fight it's going to be because we Techs won it, and if we lose it's going to be us who lost it."

He seemed to be waiting for an answer, so Lonnie said, "Yes, sir."

"Some of us think that because we're technical specialists, and our special skills make us too valuable to be risked in combat, we're too good to activate weapons when the need arises. I hope you know better."

"Sir—"

"Yes?"

"It isn't really that."

Koppel frowned. "Isn't really what?"

"All that about special skills. I mean, driving a truck—a truck that will mostly drive itself. It's because the tests showed they couldn't trust us in a fight but the public would be angry if we were deferred for that. It's not more of us they need, it's more of them."

"Daws, I think you ought to have a talk with the chaplain."

"You know it's true, sir. They only say all that so we won't resent the Marksmen so much, and even with all the propaganda, sometimes Supply won't give out things they have to Marksmen when they think they can get away with it. And last month when that mechanic in the motor pool got his foot mashed when the jack slipped, the medics let a Marksman bleed to death while they treated him."

"I am going to ask you again to talk to the chaplain, Daws. In fact, I'm going to order it. Sometime during the next three days. He'll tell me when you've come."

"Yes, sir."

"The injustices you spoke of *are* lamentable—if they actually occurred, which I doubt. But the motivation for them was the quite natural superiority felt by men who have difficulty in taking human life. The psychs know what they're doing, Daws."

"It isn't that either, sir." Something in Lonnie's throat was warning him to stop, but it was crushed by the memory of unconscious men sprawled on white gravel. "We can kill. We could kick a helpless man to death. What we can't do—"

"That will be enough! You're trying for a psycho discharge, aren't you Daws? Well, you won't get it from me. You're dismissed!"

Lonnie saluted, waited a moment more with the vague feeling that Koppel might have something further to say, then made an about-face and left the tent.

It was raining hard now. A dark figure carrying more than the usual quantity of clattering mess gear was waiting under the eaves of the Aid tent. Brewer, of course. As Lonnie stepped into the rain he came forward, the wind whipping his poncho. "Ready for chow?"

Lonnie accepted his own mess gear.

"You got a chewing out in there, huh?"

"Could you hear it?"

"It shows on your face, Lon. Don't feel bad, this weather has everybody on edge—no air."

Lonnie stared at him, feeling stupid.

"No chopper strikes because they're afraid they might hit us instead. It's got all the crumby Markies so jumpy they're shooting at each other."

When they were inside the mess tent Lonnie asked, "You think anything will happen? Maybe this is what they've been waiting for."

Brewer shook his head, accepting a turkey leg from a KP server. Marksmen ate first, but the cooks, Techs themselves, held back the best pieces and biggest portions.

"There's a lot more of them out there than there are of us," Lonnie said.

Brewer snorted. "We could get reinforcements from Corps in six hours. Maybe less—four hours."

To himself Lonnie wondered.

It began at two minutes after midnight. Lonnie knew, because when he hit the dirt beside his cot, he struck his watch against one of the legs and the humming little fork inside went silent forever, leaving the hands upraised like a stout man and a thin one clutching each other for reassurance.

It began with rockets and big mortars, each detonation shaking the wet ground and lighting the camp with its flash, even through the rain. Shouting platoons of Marksmen splashed down the Headquarters Company street outside his tent on their way to their positions, and somewhere someone was screaming.

Then their own radar-eyed, computer-directed artillery had ranged the incoming rounds and begun to fire back.

At almost the same moment, Lonnie heard the perimeter multilaunchers go into action, and flares burst overhead sending stark blue light through every crevice in the tent. He rolled under one hanging side curtain and sprinted for a sandbagged dugout nearby. It was dark and half full of water and entirely full of men, but he wedged in somehow.

No one spoke. As each rocket came whistling down he closed his eyes and, knowing how absurd it was, tensed. The blackness, the shrieking missiles and the explosions, the hip-high water and the ragged breathing of the men pressed against him seemed to endure for hours.

Abruptly, the darkness changed to dancing yellow light in which he could see the drawn faces around him. Someone with a flashlight stood in the doorway, and a voice from the back of the dugout yelled, "Turn that thing off."

Instead of obeying, the man with the light snapped, "Everybody outside. We need you at the tank park."

No one moved.

A second man appeared, and the first flicked his light on him long enough to show that he was holding an automatic rifle. "Come out," the first man said. "In a minute we're going to spray the place."

As they filed out a rocket struck somewhere to their left, and men threw themselves down in the mud in front of the dugout. Lonnie and several others did not, standing numbly erect in the firework glare of the flares while the soft earth trembled and shrapnel tore at the tents. The wind had died and the rain fell straight down, dripping from the rims of their helmets, washing the tops of their boots whenever they stood still.

When everyone was out—everyone, at least, who would obey the order to come out—the automatic rifleman fired a long burst through the doorway. Then, led by the man with the flashlight, with the automatic rifleman bringing up the rear, they started off.

The tank park had been a victim of its own design. Sheltered from surprise rockets or mortar strikes in a branch of the central valley, its one exit had been further narrowed by spider wire intended to defend it from infiltrating raiders. Now this exit was blocked by a combat car belly-deep in mud. Half a dozen men were already working to free it when they came up; the man with the flashlight, now seen to be a green-uniformed lieutenant not much older than Lonnie himself, waved his light toward a jumbled pile of tools. "Get it out. We have to bring the tanks into action or we don't have a chance. When you get it going and we can get them out, you can go back to your hole."

They worked frantically. A minim-dozer, floating on whining fans with only its thrust screws engaging the mud, leveled ruts and swept away the worst of the liquescent ooze while they drove in the suction probes of enthalpy pumps to freeze the stuff enough to give it traction. They shoved exploded aluminum mats under the combat car's churning triangular wheel assemblies and labored to lighten it by unbolting its foam-backed ceramic armor.

With a cassette of ammunition someone had flung him from the turret hatch, Lonnie stumbled through the mud—then, suddenly, lay facedown in it half deaf, a roaring in his ears and the cassette gone. He shook his head to clear it, opening and closing his mouth; the side of his face stung as though burned.

When he stood up he found his clothing had been ripped and scorched. Around him other survivors were rising as well; at their feet those who had not lived lay—some dismembered, some apparently untouched. A crater a meter deep and three meters wide gaped between the mired combat car and his own position, showing where the rocket had struck.

"Armor piercing," someone near him said. He looked around and recognized the lieutenant who had driven them from the dugout. "Armor piercing," the officer repeated half to himself. "Or it would have gone off higher up and gotten us all."

"Yes," Lonnie said.

The lieutenant looked around, noticing him. For a moment he seemed about to answer, but he shouted an order instead, to Lonnie and all the others.

Several obeyed, redoubling their efforts to free the combat car. Several merely stood staring. Two tried to help the wounded, and some others moved away from the car, the crater, and the shouting officer—moved away as inconspicuously as they could, a few walking backward, all looking for shadowed spots even darker than the rain-drenched darkness about the car.

The automatic rifleman saw one group and ran yelling toward them. They halted. Still running, the rifleman circled them until he barred their way, then—too quickly for Lonnie to see what had happened—he was down and the men he had tried to stop were jumping and stumbling across him, one carrying his rifle. The officer with the flashlight drew a pistol and fired, the shots coming so close together they sounded almost like a burst from an automatic weapon.

Lonnie was running and telling himself as he ran that it was dangerous to run, that the lieutenant with the flashlight would shoot him in the back. But by then it was too late; the tank park was somewhere behind him, and the ground beneath his pounding feet was no longer merely mud but a nightmare landscape of ditches and holes from which timbers and steel posts protruded.

Something pulled sharply and insistently at his wreck of a shirt. He stopped, turned around. There was no one there.

Something very swift passed close to his head. Stupidly, awkwardly, he got down. First to hands and knees, then prone, thinking as he did of a picnic at which he remembered lying belly-down in young grass. The thing, the bullet, had made an unvocalizable noise that was not a Voisriit BANG at all, but a sound suggesting a whip cracked very close to his ear. He thought of this as he lay in the oozing mud, and it came to him that the brief sound had in fact been hours of exposition packed into a millisecond; that it had been this compression that had made its strange rustle. It had told of Death, and he knew that he had heard and that he, who had been frightened merely by the thought of pain before—because he did not know Death—had understood. It had spoken, and the word spoken had been *never*. Never again, anything. Never again, even the luxury of being afraid. Never. Nothing.

He had seen his body, his own body, as it lay bloated and stinking; and much more . . .

His stomach was cold. He recalled being told of a fellow student at the university who had killed himself by swallowing dry ice, and thought it must have felt like that; but no, that would be flatulent as well, and he did not feel flatulent. Something splattered two meters in front, throwing up mud. The taste of brass was in his mouth.

A ditch—a trench he now realized—yawned not far to his

right; he foundered toward it and rolled in.

He could stand now if he stooped. His hands touched the trench wall and felt the bulging burlap of sandbags, dripping wet. He wondered if the man who had shot at him (he was not certain whether it had been an insurgent or a Marksman) would throw a grenade. He would not see it in the darkness, he knew. He took a step forward and put his foot upon a man's hand. It jerked away and someone groaned, the motion and sound giving the impression—gone in an instant—that he had stepped on a rabbit or a rat. He crouched and heard the bubbling of a chest wound as the man tried to breathe. His fingers groped for the wound but found instead the thick straps of a sort of harness.

"Here," the wounded man whispered. "Here."

"In a minute," Lonnie said. "Let me get this off you." Then, mostly because he found talking somehow relieved his fear, "What is it anyway?"

"Fl . . . flame . . ." A whisper.

"Never mind." The straps were held by a central buckle. With it loosed, he could slide them away from the man's chest. His aid kit contained a self-adhesive dressing, and when he had located the wound he spread it in place. The bubbling stopped and he could hear the wounded man draw deep, choking breaths. "I'll get you to the aid station if I can," Lonnie said.

Weakly the man asked, "You're not one of our lads?"

"I guess not. U.N." He picked the man up, then crouched again as a flight of flechettes whizzed overhead.

"We have you, you know," the man said.

"What?" The flechettes, steel arrows like the darts men played with in bars here, had filled his mind.

"We have you. There's thousands more of ours coming,

and my own lot almost did for you by ourselves a bit ago. Too many of yours won't fight."

Lonnie said, "The ratio's about the same on both sides —we know who ours are, that's all." He was answering with only a part of his thought, the rest concentrated on a new sound, a sound from the direction from which the flechettes had come. It was a scuffing and a breathing, the clinking of a hundred buckles and buttons against the fiberglass stocks of weapons, the husky voices of automatic rifle bolts as nervous men checked their loading by touch, then checked again. The squish of a thousand boots in mud.

"You think they can do that? Tell one lad has it and another doesn't?" The wounded man sounded genuinely curious, but there was a touch of scorn in his voice.

"Well, they examine the person and go by probabilities. They're very thorough."

"They did it to you?"

Lonnie nodded, but he was not thinking of the examination, the cold, long-wired sensors gummed to his skin. He said, "I was worrying about my mice. All the time I was answering the questions and looking at the holograph projections and everything, it was kind of in the back of my mind—you know, whether my mother would take care of them right while I was gone."

"Mice?" the wounded man asked, and then, "Here now, what're you doin'?"

"Fancy mice, with little rosettes of fur on them, and waltzing mice. I bred them." He had put the wounded man down and was running his fingers over the mechanism of the flamer the man had carried. "I remembered them just now, and I haven't thought about them for months. Now I think maybe I'd like to take them up again, if I get back.

You know a lot of progress in medicine has come from studying the genetics of mice." The flamer seemed simple: two valves already opened, tubes leading to a sort of gun like the nozzle of a gasoline pump.

"Dirty job, I should think, cleaning up after them."

Lonnie said, "If you don't clean their cages, they die." Propping the flamer against the dripping wall of the trench, he backed into the harness and pulled the straps over his shoulders.

The blade of the wounded man's knife had been blackened, but the ground edge flashed in the faint light, and Lonnie threw up his arm in time to block the blow and wrench the knife from the man's weak fingers. "If you do something like that again," he said softly, "I'm going to pull off that patch I put on your chest."

After that he stood, his eyes just higher than the top of the trench, ignoring the man. He did not have to wait long.

The insurgents came raggedly but by the hundreds, firing as they advanced. He raised himself to his full height, glancing for some reason at his watch as he straightened up. The hands still stood at two minutes past midnight, unmoving, and that he felt must be correct. It was a new day.

His gouts of orange flame, hot as molten steel, held the straggling lines back until the three tanks came; and when they did he vaulted out of the trench and jogged forward with them, keeping twenty meters ahead until the canisters on his back were as empty and light as cardboard.

Hot Potato

INTRODUCTION

War is a grim business. And nuclear bombs are the grimmest weapons that man has yet devised. So here's a lighthearted story about H-bombs and the threat to destroy not just one world, but two.

The idea of a parallel space-time, with another Earth that exists in some other set of dimensions, has been used by many SF writers. But never exactly the way Burt Filer does: he gives us Continuum Track A (our own space-time) and Continuum Track B (with a similar but yet different Earth), and the intriguing "funnyspace" in between the two tracks.

Burt Filer is a young, handsome, curly-topped, bright New Yorker who is an inventor, a mechanic par excellence, a motorcyclist, and—when he puts his considerable talents to it—a fine SF writer.

So here is a story about war, H-bombs, a parallel universe, and the undefeatable ingenuity of man.

by BURT K. FILER

SECRET BOMB STORES FOR CHINESE

Peking, May 7, 2010—UAP

Four thousand megatons of fusion weapons were transferred to a Chinese "mystery stockpile" last week, General Ho Muchun announced today. Minister of War Muchun spoke at a press luncheon here, held in the Red House Lotus Garden. He was openly optimistic when questioned about the secrecy of his nuclear arsenal. "Imperialist Yankees never find in a million years," was his smug and smiling reply.

As the present cold war standoff is based wholly on the threat of mutual sabotage, the general's comments bode ill for the U.S. Whereas the Chinese have exact knowledge of all U.S. installations, said Muchun, the reverse is no longer true. Thanks to his secret hiding place, he claims the U.S. has no retaliatory measures.

"Can't blow up what you can't find," he added philosophically.

Washington has made no immediate comment.

* tick *

"Damn, blast, hell, they've developed the timespool!" was General Galen Panhard's immediate comment. He hurled down the morning paper. "Get me Major Tucker! No—wait a minute—get the news service first."

Orderlies scattered like panicked chickens. Six telephones

were on his desk in thirty seconds and three had reached the UAP.

"Hello? This is Panhard—well, hang the other two up, fool—now, listen. We've got a secret arsenal too, and what's more it's bigger than Muchun's, and what's more we know where *his* is and he doesn't know where *ours* is. Tell the old buzzard to stuff that in (cough) his pipe and smoke it! Good-bye (slam).

"Where's Tucker? TUCK–ER-R-R!" he bellowed. "Get the car. We're going out to see Cordoba."

* tock *

In the back seat of Ford-Chrysler's biggest and blackest and latest limousine, the two men presented an odd contrast.

General Galen Panhard was a jut-jawed, big-chested man of action. In his news photos "Old Pinhead" looked 6′ 6″ and 300 pounds. Actually he was 5′ 4″ and a shade over 160, but the impression of bigness still prevailed.

Next to him sat Major Dennis Tucker. Denny was a medium-tall, well-fed man of thirty with an absolutely forgettable face. They called him Wallpaper because he blended right in. Nobody actually believed he'd taken Quanoi apart singlehanded. Nobody but Panhard, who'd been there. He'd kept Denny as his personal Staff Assistant, bodyguard, and poop-boy ever since.

They rumbled slowly through Washington's sweet morning air, across the bridge, and up into the lush Virginia countryside. Panhard fumed impatiently with eyes squinted half shut, and Denny snored quietly with his own lids down all the way. It was six A.M.

In forty minutes they arrived at Dr. Emile Cordoba's farmhouse laboratory. It wasn't a farmhouse for security's sake, oh no. Such camouflage would have been childishly transparent. It was a farmhouse because Cordoba liked farmhouses. Helped him think, he said. And as the government was very anxious to keep him thinking, a way was found to salve the scientist's idiosyncrasy. He had others.

Dr. Cordoba was a thin and serious forty-five. Beneath his black hair was a pale, handsome face that had a pipe stuck in it most of the time. Because he'd developed the timespool everyone thought Emile was smarter than hell, which was probably correct.

"Looks like someone reads the early paper," he commented, holding open the car door.

"Huh?" asked Denny, who hadn't. He stumbled out, nudged from behind by his boss.

"Don't mind this imbecile, Emile," said Panhard impatiently. "Let's go inside."

Labs are rarely attractive but this one came close. The walls were a restful russet and on the floor was a teflon rug which matched the subtly tinted window glass. Paintings hung here and there, real ones.

"What happened to the Degas ballerina?" Denny asked, noting a blank spot on the wall.

"Little accident," Emile admitted sheepishly. "Kind of blew a hole in 'er with the welding beam."

"Too bad."

They took seats around an island of equipment in the middle of the floor. Rising from a cluster of wiry filaments was a twelve-foot spool with a door in its side. Both rested on a platform of even more esoteric gadgetry.

"Question—probably rhetorical," began the general. "*Do* the Chinese have it?" He gestured at the timespool.

"Answer—equally rhetorical, judging by that news article," replied Emile, "is yes."

Light dawned in Denny's eyes. "So they're storing their weapons in another time track too," he mused, "just like us. Nice." He yawned.

"Just like us, not nice," corrected Emile. "What're we going to do about it?"

"Carry the war into the alternate continuum, of course," snapped the general. "Tucker?" he rapped at the still drowsy young major.

"Yes, sir?"

"You will go into Time Track B, find that Chinese ammo dump, and eliminate it. Just like Quanoi back in '99."

"Aw for cry—"

"That'll be all, boy."

"Boy? General, I *was* a boy back in Ninety-nine, but not anymore. Sabotage and all that stuff is so—so *uncomfortable* for a man of my years, y'know."

"TUCK—"

"YessirI'llgoI'llgoI'llgo."

Denny didn't mind getting into the space suit so much. He didn't mind wedging himself with half a dozen weapons into the spool, either. In fact the whole assignment wasn't that bad once he'd accepted it. As Emile and the general waved through the window, the bland major was primarily disconsolate about having missed breakfast.

* tick *

How many men, Denny asked himself, have ever had the privilege of getting sick on an empty stomach in quantum space? Probably just me. Maybe a Chinaman or two as well. We'll see.

The shell of "funnyspace" between what Denny regarded as the present (actually Continuum Track A) and the "alternate present" (specifically, Continuum Track B), was a horrible place. But it was a place.

Emile explained it to him once. Time was quantified and not continuous. You didn't move smoothly from track to track but went in a series of jumps, like an electron hopping from ring to ring in an atom. What's significant is that the space between is timeless. Things "are" there. Things never "were" and never "would be," they continuously "are."

Which is why the space had so many Major Denny Tuckers in it. Each time Denny went across, he left an imprint which never faded and never moved. Going through now, he saw several other spools floating nearby, each with himself inside. He waved. They never waved back. There would be two spools for each of the six round trips to B he'd already taken.

Which of course comes to twelve, but today he counted fifteen. Three were spherical instead of cylindrical, red instead of silver, and had the same funny little yellow face peeking out of them.

Peking—out of them? Of course, no doubt about it now. The Chinese were definitely ferrying fusionables into B.

Whango! Out of quantum space and into B-time, just as rough as usual. Why didn't Emile fix that? Undogging the hatch, Denny drifted out into real space.

He'd been transported physically as well as temporally. Instead of arriving in the B-world's equivalent of Cordoba's farmhouse, he'd been deposited in orbit around the planet. Emile had frankly admitted ignorance of what conditions on the surface of track B's earth would be like, but decided it would be better to avoid the complications of finding out. Just go, leave the bombs in orbit, and come back.

Not thirty yards away bobbed a loose pile of atomic explosives Denny'd ferried out on previous runs. This time his mission was different, he reminded himself.

Emile had suggested Denny hunt through the East-West orbits near his own for the Chinese ammo dump. It was almost too easy. A quick scan through his faceplate binoculars showed the chubby red spool not twenty miles away.

Dennis Tucker was no astronaut. Until he pulled this last lousy tour of duty with Old Pinhead, he hadn't even been to the moon. So he should be forgiven for turning up the wick on his pocket rocket a bit too high.

Attempting to sneak up on the Chinaman, he instead overshot by a couple of miles. As Denny drifted past, the amazed Oriental did a fast double take and scrambled toward his round red spool.

Well, what the hell, Denny thought, maybe I can get him from here. Putting his rocket on retro, he shouldered the M110 and tried to lay a beam on the excited figure behind. He missed, deceleration throwing him off. Then an answering flash of brilliance sizzled just past his ear.

Why you nasty, Denny growled. You've got a gun, too. He squeezed off another beam, which sent the enemy soldier scuttling behind a large pile of crates floating near his spool. Fusion weapons, Denny supposed. Hmmm. Well, why not, he mused with a devil-may-care grin. I'm in the open and he's not. He'll pick me off any minute. If I'm going to go, I might as well get the job done. He centered the muzzle of his M110 on the deadly heap.

"*Hold* it, Buster!" said an eerily familiar voice over his own QL circuit. "Just what in hell d'you think you're doing?" A heavy hand thumped Denny none too gently from behind. Startled is an inadequate word.

"Why, ah, I'm making the world safe for democracy," he stammered. The hand on his shoulder was joined by another and Denny was spun roughly around.

He confronted—himself. Oh, the man wasn't an exact copy and his space suit looked a little more sophisticated, but there, floating two feet away over the world of track B, was a guy whose name just had to be Dennis Tucker.

"*Whose* world?" asked the pugnacious B-Denny. "You guys've got colossal nerve, y'know it? How'd you like it if we set off those babies over *your* earth, eh? How'd you like that?"

"Not too much, I suppose. Er, don't you think we'd better hide? There's a Chinese over there with a gun and—"

"Don't worry about him," snapped B-Denny, "worry about me. My buddy's got a pistol like this one on him."

Denny turned. Sure enough, there were two figures floating together back there, seemingly engaged in animated conversation. Directly overhead were two spools very much like his own.

"Can't we talk this over?"

"We *are* talking it over," snapped B-Denny with a wave of his sidearm. "It's simple. Get out of here and take your damn bombs with you. *We* don't want 'em. Hell, man, you think maybe there isn't an East-West war on over here, too? Why, if *our* Chinese ever found— Never mind, you know how it works. Now let's go."

"Yes, sir."

Denny rocketed back to his spool and loaded as much of the fusionable stores as he could into it. His opposite number kept a careful guard on him. Reasonable, Denny thought. I wouldn't trust me either.

"Now hustle right back for the rest of this junk," said

B-Denny. "I'll wait for you. And don't let Old Pinhead talk you into any tricks. Remember, pal, I've got a General Panhard breathing down my neck, too. So long."

Denny nodded an unhappy farewell and punched "RETURN." The timespool jolted, and there he was back in funnyspace.

"Crud and corruption," Denny muttered aloud. "Pinhead isn't going to like this at *all!*"

* tock *

"Tuck-er-rr! How could you? How *could* you? Don't you realize you've jeopardized our entire mode of defense? Now put that bomb back in the spool and take it right back. You hear me, Major?"

"But those people. That other world—"

"Forget 'em, damn it. Emile says they don't exist."

"Is that true, Emile?" Denny asked from the edge of the platform, where he'd been cornered since returning five minutes earlier. Panhard had confronted him from the floor below and wouldn't let him down. The tough little general's face was scarlet and his fists were a tight contrasting white on his hips.

Two paces behind him stood Emile Cordoba with his own hands deep in the pockets of a gray lab coat. He looked worried.

"Not objectively, no, they don't," answered the scientist. "But that's because they're not within our own objective space. *We* don't exist for them either, until—"

"Until when?" asked Panhard, turning.

"Until we intrude into their objective world. Actually, General, this is a touchy situation and I—"

"Bull. Get going, Tucker. That's an order!"

"Yes, sir."

* tick *

B-Denny was waiting, gun in hand.

"Well, that was fast. Ready for another load?"

"Not exactly," Denny said sheepishly. "Pinhead made me bring it back."

"What! Listen, stupid, you're a nice guy and all that but I've been instructed to use 'force necessary.' You know what that means?"

Denny shoved off from the spool and drifted over to his B-twin. "Let's go down and talk to *your* General Panhard. Maybe he'll be easier to deal with than mine," he said reasonably.

"You're dreaming. But what the hell, I guess you could give it a try. Follow me." B-Denny holstered his pistol.

Cramming themselves into the B-timespool, Denny felt the familiar jolt of temporal discontinuity, spent two seconds in a different kind of funnyspace than he was used to, and found himself back in Cordoba's lab. B-Cordoba's lab.

"Very nice," he commented as they stepped out. "Didn't know you could use these for ordinary transportation. Right down from orbit."

"We're a little ahead of you all around," said B-Denny, "or we'd never have detected your atomic cache up there in the first—"

"Tuck-k-k-ker!" bellowed General B-Panhard. They both blanched. "Which the hell of you is which? Oh. You, A-Tucker, listen up. You're a menace and we ought to fry you. Take those bombs back or we *will* fry you."

"Sir," Denny began, metering his words carefully because he knew he'd only get to say about five, "can't you appreciate the stalemate we're in?"

The jut-jaw opened, then shut. "Yes," he said tiredly,

"yes, I can. Sit down, boy. Both of you." They dropped to the edge of the platform, legs dangling over. B-Emile was there but kept silent. Pulling up a tall lab stool, the little warrior perched on it like a bantam rooster.

"First of all, A-Tucker, it's not a stalemate. Track B is several decades more advanced scientifically than A, physical similarities notwithstanding. If we *really* got tough we could hang a time fuse on all those bombs and send 'em back to you—detonating. Ever think of that? But you're human even though you're not objectively real, and we don't want your blood on our hands.

"Now look, son, I know it's tough. You're in the middle, the hot potato that nobody loves. I've given it to y'straight. We're trying to be decent, but you take those bombs back or else. Work it out with your own General Panhard."

Denny remained silent after the other finished, hopelessly silent. This Panhard was more enlightened but just as stubborn as his own. B-Emile finally spoke.

"General," he began cautiously, "there're a few implications here I'm beginning to worry about. Now that track A's got the timespool, we should expect to see a lot more of them. Major Tucker here could be a preliminary envoy. Perhaps we can work out something more definite, possibly a little less, ah, strongly worded? After all, it wouldn't do to—"

"Bull," scoffed B-Panhard. "We're in the driver's seat, aren't we? They do what we say or pow!"

Oh, my aging Uncle Fred, Denny thought bleakly to himself, it all sounds *so* familiar.

An hour later B-Denny had taken him back up to the orbit of his spool, helped him load, and seen him off.

* tock *

"Back!" shrieked his own General Panhard. "I don't care what they say, Tucker, take the blasted bomb back. If those nonexistent nobodies think they've got a technical edge on us, they'll damn well have to prove it. We'll take 'em on any time!"

"But, sir, they've threatened to—"

A pistol beam sizzled past Denny's ear and burnt a hole in another painting in Emile's lab. Pinhead was verging on apoplexy. Emile, still standing a pace or two behind the general, just shrugged helplessly.

"Baackabackbabababb—" chattered the frenzied warrior, raising his weapon again.

"Yes, sir."

* tick *

Well, here I am back in funnyspace, soon to be the first casualty of the first temporal war. Great. B-Emile was right, intercontinuum relations are off to a bad start. As a matter of fact I begin to think they're going to be perpetually, miserably hopeless. Which reminds me of Quanoi a little bit.

Hmmm.

* tock *

Back to Time Track B. The other Denny and a small army in space suits confronted him as he stepped out. Behind them was an oversize timespool. Saying not one word, they electrostunned him into unconsciousness.

He awoke in a cast of rigid plastic foam, completely immobilized. Where was—oh, yes, inside the big spool. Around him was piled every piece of nuclear hardware he'd ever brought over from A, plus some extras. The Chinese stuff of course. Next to him was his Oriental dueling partner of a few hours earlier, wrapped in a similar foam cocoon.

B-Denny was standing in the hatchway, apparently giving the stowage a final inspection. Drawing a small, egg-shaped time fuse from his chestpack, he carefully set it, then tossed it on the deck a dozen feet from his captives.

"S'long," said B-Denny with just a hint of sadness. "Sorry to have to blow up your world along with you."

"Wait," Denny called. "C'mere a minute. I've got the answer to this whole mess."

Outside the big spool, B-Denny's detachment of soldiers waited impatiently. They were surprised to see both Dennis Tuckers emerge and together shut the hatch. Had that non-existent phony from A-track conned the major into something, or what?

As the big cylinder flickered off into quantum space, the soldiers overheard a brief conversation on the QL circuit.

"Great idea," said B-Denny. "Simple, too."

"Thanks."

"Only one thing, pal," the B-twin went on as they turned to rejoin his men. "Always felt that one of me was more than Old Pinhead could cheerfully tolerate. With *two* of us around here from now on—"

* tick *

Back in track A, two men waited.

"Well, Cordoba, where's the spool and where's Tucker?"

"Don't know, General. How long's it been now, six hours? It's dangerous but I could recall the spool. Denny might not be in it, though, and—"

"Recall it."

"Okay, General," sighed the scientist. Going up to the cluster of instruments on the platform, Cordoba did little things to little things. There was a hum.

Blink.

"What was that," Old Pinhead asked impatiently, "a flashbulb? Where's the spool?"

"Should be here," Emile muttered. "Isn't though, is it? Hmmm."

"Well?"

"Tell you what, General. I've got a spare spool. I'll go take a look for him."

* tick tock bong *

So Emile Cordoba carefully stuck his nose into the quantum space between tracks A and B. For a few microseconds only.

His spool blinked back on the platform with its hull red hot. The hatch flew open and he burst out yipping and hopping, rubbing blistered hands that had touched the hatch handle, and kicking off shoes with charred soles. And though in what must have been severe pain, the slender scientist was grinning from ear to ear.

"Wow," he gasped from the floor. "That really wraps it up. No more continuum hopping."

"What!" asked the startled Panhard. "Here, Emile, those hands look bad, let me—"

"No, I'll be okay. But you won't, my friend. You remember about the perpetualness of events in quantum space?"

"Yes, yes of course—"

"Well, General," giggled Emile Cordoba as shock wafted him off into unconsciousness. "There's a big ball of hell hanging in there that's never going to leave. Not ever. We're locked into A forever. Old smart-alec Tucker's closed the door between us and any other continuum track. He's gone and H-bombed funnyspace!"

All Cats Are Gray

INTRODUCTION

There's a mistaken belief that science fiction is entirely a man's province. This, despite the fact that SF's many worlds include a generous share of stories by a goodly-sized number of lovely and talented women.

Among the best of them is Andre Norton, who is well known as the author of very successful juvenile novels that range through the worlds of SF, fantasy, and mystery. Among her most recent books are Ice Crown, Dread Companion, *and* High Sorcery. *A former librarian and bookshop manager, Miss Norton has won a large hatful of awards, and her work has been translated into more than a dozen foreign languages.*

*Here, in "*All Cats Are Gray,*" she brings together a striking female protagonist, an invisible villain, and a tough old tomcat. All are drawn in a deft, compact style that doesn't waste a word.*

by ANDRE NORTON

STEENA of the Spaceways—that sounds just like a corny title for one of the Stellar-Vedo spreads. I ought to know, I've tried my hand at writing enough of them. Only this Steena was no glamorous babe. She was as colorless as a lunar planet—even the hair netted down to her skull had a sort of grayish cast, and I never saw her but once draped in anything but a shapeless and baggy gray spaceall.

Steena was strictly background stuff, and that is where she mostly spent her free hours—in the smelly, smoky, background corners of any stellar-port dive frequented by free spacers. If you really looked for her you could spot her—just sitting there listening to the talk—listening and remembering. She didn't open her own mouth often. But when she did, spacers had learned to listen. And the lucky few who heard her rare spoken words—these will never forget Steena.

She drifted from port to port. Being an expert operator on the big calculators, she found jobs wherever she cared to stay for a time. And she came to be something like the masterminded machines she tended—smooth, gray, without much personality of their own.

But it was Steena who told Bub Nelson about the Jovan moon rites—and her warning saved Bub's life six months later. It was Steena who identified the piece of stone Keene Clark was passing around a table one night, rightly calling it unworked Slitite. That started a rush which made ten fortunes overnight for men who were down to their last jets. And, last of all, she cracked the case of the *Empress of Mars*.

All the boys who had profited by her queer store of knowledge and her photographic memory tried at one time or another to balance the scales. But she wouldn't take so much as a cup of canal water at their expense, let alone the credits they tried to push on her. Bub Nelson was the only one who got around her refusal. It was he who brought her Bat.

About a year after the Jovan affair, he walked into the Free Fall one night and dumped Bat down on her table. Bat looked at Steena and growled. She looked calmly back at him and nodded once. From then on they traveled together—the thin gray woman and the big gray tomcat. Bat learned to know the inside of more stellar bars than even most spacers visit in their lifetimes. He developed a liking for Vernal juice, drank it neat and quick, right out of a glass. And he was always at home on any table where Steena elected to drop him.

This is really the story of Steena, Bat, Cliff Moran, and the *Empress of Mars*, a story which is already a legend of the spaceways. And it's a damn good story, too. I ought to know, having framed the first version of it myself.

For I was there, right in the Rigel Royal, when it all began on the night that Cliff Moran blew in, looking lower than an antman's belly and twice as nasty. He'd had a spell of luck foul enough to twist a man into a slug snake, and we all knew that there was an attachment out for his ship.

Cliff had fought his way up from the back courts of Venaport. Lose his ship and he'd slip back there—to rot. He was at the snarling stage that night when he picked out a table for himself and set out to drink away his troubles.

However, just as the first bottle arrived, so did a visitor. Steena came out of her corner, Bat curled around her shoulders stolewise, his favorite mode of travel. She crossed over and dropped down, without invitation, at Cliff's side. That shook him out of his sulks. Because Steena never chose company when she could be alone. If one of the man-stones on Ganymede had come stumping in, it wouldn't have made more of us look out of the corners of our eyes.

She stretched out one long-fingered hand, set aside the bottle he had ordered, and said only one thing, "It's about time for the *Empress of Mars* to appear."

Cliff scowled and bit his lip. He was tough, tough as jet lining—you have to be granite inside and out to struggle up from Venaport to a ship command. But we could guess what was running through his mind at that moment. The *Empress of Mars* was just about the biggest prize a spacer could aim for. But in the fifty years she had been following her queer derelict orbit through space, many men had tried to bring her in—and none had succeeded.

A pleasure ship carrying untold wealth, she had been mysteriously abandoned in space by passengers and crew, none of whom had ever been seen or heard of again. At intervals thereafter she had been sighted, even boarded. Those who ventured into her either vanished or returned swiftly without any believable explanation of what they had seen—wanting only to get away from her as quickly as possible. But the man who could bring her in—or even strip her clean in space—that man would win the jackpot.

"All right!" Cliff slammed his fist down on the table. "I'll try even that!"

Steena looked at him, much as she must have looked at Bat the day Bub Nelson brought him to her, and nodded. That was all I saw. The rest of the story came to me in pieces, months later and in another port half the system away.

Cliff took off that night. He was afraid to risk waiting—with a writ out that could pull the ship from under him. And it wasn't until he was in space that he discovered his passengers—Steena and Bat. We'll never know what happened then. I'm betting that Steena made no explanation at all. She wouldn't.

It was the first time she had decided to cash in on her own tip and she was there—that was all. Maybe that point weighed with Cliff, maybe he just didn't care. Anyway, the three were together when they sighted the *Empress* riding, her dead-lights gleaming, a ghost ship in night space.

She must have been an eerie sight because her other lights were on too, in addition to the red warnings at her nose. She seemed alive, a Flying Dutchman of space. Cliff worked his ship skillfully alongside and had no trouble in snapping magnetic lines to her lock. Some minutes later the three of them passed into her. There was still air in her cabins and corridors, air that bore a faint corrupt taint which set Bat to sniffing greedily and could be picked up even by the less sensitive human nostrils.

Cliff headed straight for the control cabin, but Steena and Bat went prowling. Closed doors were a challenge to both of them and Steena opened each as she passed, taking a quick look at what lay within. The fifth door opened on a room which no woman could leave without further investigation.

I don't know who had been housed there when the *Empress* left port on her last lengthy cruise. Anyone really curious can check back on the old photo-reg cards. But there was a lavish display of silk trailing out of two travel kits on the floor, a dressing table crowded with crystal and jeweled containers, along with other lures for the female which drew Steena in. She was standing in front of the dressing table when she glanced into the mirror—glanced into it and froze.

Over her right shoulder she could see the spider-silk cover on the bed. Right in the middle of that sheer, gossamer expanse was a sparkling heap of gems, the dumped contents of some jewel case. Bat had jumped to the foot of the bed and flattened out as cats will, watching those gems, watching them and—something else!

Steena put out her hand blindly and caught up the nearest bottle. As she unstoppered it, she watched the mirrored bed. A gemmed bracelet rose from the pile, rose in the air and tinkled its siren song. It was as if an idle hand played . . . Bat spat almost noiselessly. But he did not retreat. Bat had not yet decided his course.

She put down the bottle. Then she did something which perhaps few of the men she had listened to through the years could have done. She moved without hurry or sign of disturbance on a tour about the room. And, although she approached the bed, she did not touch the jewels. She could not force herself to do that. It took her five minutes to play out her innocence and unconcern. Then it was Bat who decided the issue.

He leaped from the bed and escorted something to the

door, remaining a careful distance behind. Then he mewed loudly twice. Steena followed him and opened the door wider.

Bat went straight on down the corridor, as intent as a hound on the warmest of scents. Steena strolled behind him, holding her pace to the unhurried gait of an explorer. What sped before them was invisible to her, but Bat was never baffled by it.

They must have gone into the control cabin almost on the heels of the unseen—if the unseen had heels, which there was a good reason to doubt—for Bat crouched just within the doorway and refused to move on. Steena looked down the length of the instrument panels and officers' station seats to where Cliff Moran worked. Her boots made no sound on the heavy carpet, and he did not glance up but sat humming through set teeth, as he tested the tardy and reluctant responses to buttons which had not been pushed in years.

To human eyes they were alone in the cabin. But Bat still followed a moving something, which he had at last made up his mind to distrust and dislike. For now he took a step or two forward and spat—his loathing made plain by every raised hair along his spine. And in that same moment Steena saw a flicker—a flicker of vague outline against Cliff's hunched shoulders, as if the invisible one had crossed the space between them.

But why had it been revealed against Cliff and not against the back of one of the seats or against the panels, the walls of the corridor or the cover of the bed where it had reclined and played with its loot? What could Bat see?

The storehouse memory that had served Steena so well

through the years clicked open a half-forgotten door. With one swift motion, she tore loose her spaceall and flung the baggy garment across the back of the nearest seat.

Bat was snarling now, emitting the throaty rising cry that was his hunting song. But he was edging back, back toward Steena's feet, shrinking from something he could not fight but which he faced defiantly. If he could draw it after him, past that dangling spaceall . . . He had to—it was their only chance!

"What the . . ." Cliff had come out of his seat and was staring at them.

What he saw must have been weird enough: Steena, bare-armed and bare-shouldered, her usually stiffly-netted hair falling wildly down her back; Steena watching empty space with narrowed eyes and set mouth, calculating a single wild chance. Bat, crouched on his belly, was retreating from thin air step by step and wailing like a demon.

"Toss me your blaster." Steena gave the order calmly—as if they still sat at their table in the Rigel Royal.

And as quietly, Cliff obeyed. She caught the small weapon out of the air with a steady hand—caught and leveled it.

"Stay just where you are!" she warned. "Back, Bat, bring it back!"

With a last throat-splitting screech of rage and hate, Bat twisted to safety between her boots. She pressed with thumb and forefinger, firing at the spacealls. The material turned to powdery flakes of ash—except for certain bits which still flapped from the scorched seat—as if something had protected them from the force of the blast. Bat sprang straight up in the air with a scream that tore their ears.

"What . . . ?" began Cliff again.

Steena made a warning motion with her left hand. "*Wait!*"

She was still tense, still watching Bat. The cat dashed madly around the cabin twice, running crazily with white-ringed eyes and flecks of foam on his muzzle. Then he stopped abruptly in the doorway, stopped and looked back over his shoulder for a long, silent moment. He sniffed delicately.

Steena and Cliff could smell it too now, a thick oily stench which was not the usual odor left by an exploding blaster shell.

Bat came back, treading daintily across the carpet, almost on the tips of his paws. He raised his head as he passed Steena, and then he went confidently beyond to sniff, to sniff and spit twice at the unburned strips of the spaceall. Having thus paid his respects to the late enemy, he sat down calmly and set to washing his fur with deliberation. Steena sighed once and dropped into the navigator's seat.

"Maybe now you'll tell me what in the hell's happened?" Cliff exploded as he took the blaster out of her hand.

"Gray," she said dazedly, "it must have been gray—or I couldn't have seen it like that. I'm color-blind, you see. I can see only shades of gray—my whole world is gray. Like Bat's—his world is gray, too—all gray. But he's been compensated, for he can see above and below our range of color vibrations and, apparently, so can I!"

Her voice quavered, and she raised her chin with a new air Cliff had never seen before—a sort of proud acceptance. She pushed back her wandering hair, but she made no move to imprison it under the heavy net again.

"That is why I saw the thing when it crossed between us.

Against your spaceall it was another shade of gray—an outline. So I put out mine and waited for it to show against that—it was our only chance, Cliff.

"It was curious at first, I think, and it knew we couldn't see it—which is why it waited to attack. But when Bat's actions gave it away, it moved. So I waited to see that flicker against the spaceall, and then I let him have it. It's really very simple. . . ."

Cliff laughed a bit shakily. "But what *was* this gray thing. I don't get it."

"I think it was what made the *Empress* a derelict. Something out of space, maybe, or from another world somewhere." She waved her hands. "It's invisible because it's a color beyond our range of sight. It must have stayed in here all these years. And it kills—it must—when its curiosity is satisfied." Swiftly she described the scene, the scene in the cabin, and the strange behavior of the gem pile which had betrayed the creature to her.

Cliff did not return his blaster to its holder. "Any more of them on board, d'you think?" He didn't look pleased at the prospect.

Steena turned to Bat. He was paying particular attention to the space between two front toes in the process of a complete bath. "I don't think so. But Bat will tell us if there are. He can see them clearly, I believe."

But there weren't any more and two weeks later, Cliff, Steena, and Bat brought the *Empress* into the lunar quarantine station. And that is the end of Steena's story because, as we have been told, happy marriages need no chronicles. Steena had found someone who knew of her gray world and did not find it too hard to share with her—someone besides Bat. It turned out to be a real love match.

The last time I saw her, she was wrapped in a flame-red cloak from the looms of Rigel and wore a fortune in Jovan rubies blazing on her wrists. Cliff was flipping a three-figure credit bill to a waiter. And Bat had a row of Vernal juice glasses set up before him. Just a little family party out on the town.

The Law-Twister Shorty

INTRODUCTION

In most science fiction stories, alien creatures are either puzzling, menacing, or downright hostile. In Gordon Dickson's stories, the aliens are usually delightful.

Gordy (as he's known to all) was born in Canada. He entered the University of Minnesota at fifteen to work toward a degree in creative writing. World War II intervened and he spent three years in military service. He returned to Minnesota to get his degree, and he's been writing full time ever since leaving school. His "Soldier, Ask Not" won the science fiction fans' Hugo Award for 1965, and "Call Him Lord" received a Nebula Award from the Science Fiction Writers of America.

At science fiction conventions, Gordy can usually be found late at night in the midst of a group of bleary-eyed bystanders, leading them through the folk songs of many [illegible]. Back home in Minnesota, though, most of his time is spent turning out stories such as this one, about ten-foot-tall bearlike creatures who have [illegible] good will, and a [illegible] of fun.

The Law-Twister Shorty

INTRODUCTION

In most science fiction stories, alien creatures are either puzzling, menacing, or downright hostile. In Gordon Dickson's stories, the aliens are usually delightful.

Gordie (as he's known to all) was born in Canada. He entered the University of Minnesota at fifteen to work toward a degree in creative writing. World War II intervened, and he spent three years in military service. He returned to Minnesota to get his degree, and he's been writing full-time ever since leaving school. His "Soldier, Ask Not" won the science fiction fans' Hugo Award for 1964, and "Call Him Lord" received a Nebula Award from the Science Fiction Writers of America.

At science fiction conventions, Gordie can usually be found late at night in the midst of a group of bleary-eyed troubadors, leading them through the folk songs of many nations. Back home in Minnesota, though, most of his time is spent turning out stories such as this one, about ten-foot-tall bearlike creatures, who have intelligence, wit, and a lot of fun.

by GORDON R. DICKSON

HE'S a pretty tough character, that Iron Bender—" said the Hill Bluffer, conversationally. Malcolm O'Keefe clung to the straps of the saddle he rode on the Hill Bluffer's back, as the nearly ten-foot-tall Dilbian strode surefootedly along the narrow mountain trail, looking something like a slim Kodiak bear on his hind legs. "But a Shorty like you, Law-Twister, ought to be able to handle him, all right."

"Law-Twister . . ." echoed Mal, dizzily. The Right Honorable Joshua Guy, Ambassador Plenipotentiary to Dilbia, had said something about the Dilbians wasting no time in pinning a name of their own invention on every Shorty (as humans were called by them) they met. But Mal had not expected to be named so soon. And what was that other name the Dilbian postman carrying him had just mentioned?

"Who won't I have any trouble with, did you say?" Mal added.

"Iron Bender," said the Hill Bluffer, with a touch of impatience. "Clan Water Gap's harnessmaker. Didn't Little Bite back there at Humrog Town tell you anything about Iron Bender?"

"I . . . I think so," said Mal. Little Bite, as Ambassador Guy was known to the Dilbians, had in fact told Mal a great many things. But thinking back on their conversation now, it did not seem to Mal that the Ambassador had been very helpful in spite of all his words. "Iron Bender's the—er—protector of this Gentle . . . Gentle . . ."

"Gentle Maiden. Hor!" The Bluffer broke into an unexplained snort of laughter. "Well, anyway, that's who Iron Bender's protector of."

"And she's the one holding the three Shorties captive—"

"Captive? What're you talking about, Law-Twister?" demanded the Bluffer. "She's *adopted* them! Little Bite must have told you that."

"Well, he . . ." Mal let the words trail off. His head was still buzzing from the hypnotraining he had been given on his way to Dilbia, to teach him the language and the human-known facts about the outsize natives of this Earth-like world; and the briefing he had gotten from Ambassador Guy had only confused him further.

". . . Three tourists, evidently," Guy had said, puffing on a heavy-bowled pipe. He was a brisk little man in his sixties, with sharp blue eyes. "Thought they could slip down from the cruise by spaceliner they were taking and duck into a Dilbian village for a firsthand look at the locals. Probably had no idea what they were getting into."

"What—uh," asked Mal, "were they getting into, if I can ask?"

"Restricted territory! Treaty territory!" snapped Guy, knocking the dottle out of his pipe and beginning to refill it. Mal coughed discreetly as the fumes reached his nose. "In this sector of space we're in open competition with a race of aliens called Hemnoids, for every available, habitable world. Dilbia's a plum. But it's got this intelligent—if primitive—native race on it. Result, we've got a treaty with the

Hemnoids restricting all but emergency contact with the Dilbians—by them or us—until the Dilbians themselves become civilized enough to choose either us or the Hemnoids for interstellar partners. Highly illegal, those three tourists just dropping in like that."

"How about me?" asked Mal.

"You? You're being sent in under special emergency orders to get them out before the Hemnoids find out they've been there," said Guy. "As long as they're gone when the Hemnoids hear about this, we can duck any treaty violation charge. But you've got to get them into their shuttle boat and back into space by midnight tonight—"

The dapper little ambassador pointed outside the window of the log building that served as the human embassy on Dilbia at the dawn sunlight on the cobblestoned Humrog Street.

"Luckily, we've got the local postman in town at the moment," Guy went on. "We can mail you to Clan Water Gap with him—"

"But," Mal broke in on the flow of words, "you still haven't explained—why me? I'm just a high school senior on a work-study visit to the Pleiades. Or at least, that's where I was headed when they told me my travel orders had been picked up, and I was drafted to come here instead, on emergency duty. There must be lots of people older than I am, who're experienced—"

"Not the point in this situation," said Guy, puffing clouds of smoke from his pipe toward the log rafters overhead. "Dilbia's a special case. Age and experience don't help here as much as a certain sort of—well—personality. The Dilbian psychological profile and culture is tricky. It needs to be matched by a human with just the proper profile and character, himself. Without those natural advantages the best of age, education, and experience doesn't help in dealing with the Dilbians."

"But," said Mal, desperately, "there must be some advice you can give me—some instructions. Tell me what I ought to do, for example—"

"No, no. Just the opposite," said Guy. "We want you to follow your instincts. Do what seems best as the situation arises. You'll make out all right. We've already had a couple of examples of people who did, when they had the same kind of personality pattern you have. The book anthropologists and psychologists are completely baffled by these Dilbians as I say, but you just keep your head and follow your instincts. . . ."

He had continued to talk, to Mal's mind, making less and less sense as he went, until the arrival of the Hill Bluffer had cut the conversation short. Now, here Mal was—with no source of information left, but the Bluffer, himself.

"This, er, Iron Bender," he said to the Dilbian postman. "You were saying I ought to be able to handle him all right?"

"Well, if you're any kind of a Shorty at all," said the Bluffer, cheerfully. "There's still lots of people in these mountains, and even down in the lowlands, who don't figure a Shorty can take on a real man and win. But not me. After all, I've been tied up with you Shorties almost from the start. It was me delivered the Half-Pint Posted to the Streamside Terror. Hor! Everybody thought the Terror'd tear the Half-Pint apart. And you can guess who won, being a Shorty yourself."

"The Half-Pint Posted won?"

"Hardly worked up a sweat doing it, either," said the Hill

Bluffer. "Just like the Pick-and-Shovel Shorty, a couple of years later. Pick-and-Shovel, he took on Bone Breaker, the lowland outlaw chief—of course, Bone Breaker being a lowlander, they two tangled with swords and shields and that sort of modern junk."

Mal clung to the straps supporting the saddle on which he rode below the Hill Bluffer's massive, swaying shoulders.

"Hey!" said the Hill Bluffer, after a long moment of silence. "You go to sleep up there, or something?"

"Asleep?" Mal laughed, a little hollowly. "No. Just thinking. Just wondering where a couple of fighters like this Half-Pint and Pick-and-Shovel could have come from back on our Shorty worlds."

"Never knew them, did you?" asked the Bluffer. "I've noticed that. Most of you Shorties don't seem to know much about each other."

"What did they look like?" Mal asked.

"Well . . . you know," said the Bluffer. "Like Shorties. All you Shorties look alike, anyway. Little, squeaky-voiced characters. Like you—only, maybe not quite so skinny."

"Skinny?" Mal had spent the last year of high school valiantly lifting weights and had finally built up his five-foot-eleven frame from a hundred and forty-eight to a hundred and seventy pounds. Not that this made him any mass of muscle—particularly compared to nearly a half-ton of Dilbian. Only, he had been rather proud of the fact that he had left skinniness behind him. Now, what he was hearing was incredible! What kind of supermen had the computer found on these two previous occasions—humans who could outwrestle a Dilbian or best one of the huge native aliens with sword and shield?

On second thought, it just wasn't possible there could be

two such men, even if they had been supermen, by human standards. There had to have been some kind of a gimmick in each case that had let the humans win. Maybe, a concealed weapon of some kind—a tiny tranquilizer gun, or some such. . . .

But Ambassador Guy had been adamant about refusing to send Mal out with any such equipment.

"Absolutely against the Treaty. Absolutely!" the little ambassador had said.

Mal snorted to himself. If anyone, Dilbian or human, was under the impression that *he* was going to get into any kind of physical fight with any Dilbian—even the oldest, weakest, most midget Dilbian on the planet—they had better think again. How he had come to be selected for this job, anyway . . .

"Well, here we are—Clan Water Gap Territory!" announced the Hill Bluffer cheerfully, slowing his pace.

Mal straightened up in the saddle and looked around him. They had finally left the narrow mountain trail that had kept his heart in his mouth most of the trip. Now they had emerged into a green, bowl-shaped valley, with a cluster of log huts at its lowest point and the silver thread of a narrow river spilling into it from the valley's far end, to wind down into a lake by the huts.

But he had little time to examine the further scene in detail. Just before them, and obviously waiting in a little grassy hollow by an egg-shaped granite boulder, were four large Dilbians and one small one.

Correction—Mal squinted against the afternoon sun. Waiting by the stone were two large and one small male Dilbians, all with the graying fur of age, and one unusually tall and black-furred Dilbian female. The Hill Bluffer snorted appreciatively at the female as he carried Mal up to confront the four.

"Grown even a bit more yet, since I last saw you, Gentle Maiden," said the native postman, agreeably. "Done a pretty good job of it, too. Here, meet the Law-Twister Shorty."

"I don't want to meet him!" snapped Gentle Maiden. "And you can turn around and take him right back where you got him. He's not welcome in Clan Water Gap Territory; and I've got the Clan Grandfather here to tell him so!"

Mal's hopes suddenly took an upturn.

"Oh?" he said. "Not welcome? That's too bad. I guess there's nothing left but to go back. Bluffer—"

"Hold on, Law-Twister!" growled the Bluffer. "Don't let Gentle here fool you." He glared at the three male Dilbians. "What Grandfather? I see three grandpas—Grandpa Tricky, Grandpa Forty Winks and—" he fastened his gaze on the smallest of the elderly males, "old One Punch, here. But none of them are Grandfathers, last I heard."

"What of it?" demanded Gentle Maiden. "Next Clan meeting, the Clan's going to choose a Grandfather. One of these grandpas is going to be the one chosen. So with all three of them here, I've got the next official Grandfather of Clan Water Gap here, too—even if he doesn't know it himself, yet!"

"Hor!" The Bluffer exploded into snorts of laughter. "Pretty sneaky, Gentle, but it won't work! A Grandfather's no good until he's *named* a Grandfather. Why, if you could do things that way, we'd have little kids being put up to give Grandfather rulings. And if it came to that, where'd the point be in having a man live long enough to get wise and trusted enough to be named a Grandfather?"

He shook his head.

"No, no," he said. "You've got no real Grandfather here, and so there's nobody can tell an honest little Shorty like the Law-Twister to turn about and light out from Clan Territory."

"Told y'so, Gentle," said the shortest grandpa in a rusty voice. "Said it wouldn't work."

"You!" cried Gentle Maiden, wheeling on him. "A fine grandpa you are, One Punch—let alone the fact you're my own real, personal grandpa! You don't have to be a Grandfather! You could just tell this Shorty and this long-legged postman on your own—tell them to get out while they were still in one piece! You would have, once!"

"Well, once, maybe," said the short Dilbian, rustily and sadly. Now that Mal had a closer look at him, he saw that this particular oldster—the one the Hill Bluffer had called One Punch—bore more than a few signs of having led an active life. A number of old scars seamed his fur; one ear was only half there and the other was badly tattered. Also, his left leg was crooked as if it had been broken and badly set at one time.

"I don't see why you can't *still* do it—for your granddaughter's sake!" said Gentle Maiden sharply. Mal winced. Gentle Maiden might be good looking by Dilbian standards—the Hill Bluffer's comments a moment ago seemed to indicate that—but whatever else she was, she was plainly not very gentle, at least, in any ordinary sense of the word.

"Why, Granddaughter," creaked One Punch mildly, "like I've told you and everyone else, now that I'm older I've seen the foolishness of all those little touches of temper I used to have when I was young. They never really proved anything—except how much wiser those big men were who used to kind of avoid tangling with me. That's what comes with age, Granddaughter. Wisdom. You never hear nowdays of One Man getting into hassles, now that he's put a few years on him—or of More Jam, down there in the lowlands, talking about defending his wrestling championship anymore."

"Hold on! Wait a minute, One Punch," rumbled the Hill Bluffer. "You know and I know that even if One Man and More Jam do go around *saying* they're old and feeble nowdays, no one in his right mind is going to take either one of them at their word and risk finding out if it is true."

"Think so if you like, Postman," said One Punch, shaking his head mournfully. "Believe that if you want to. But when you're my age, you'll know it's just wisdom, plain, pure wisdom, makes men like them and me so peaceful. Besides, Gentle," he went on, turning again to his granddaughter, "you've got a fine young champion in Iron Bender—"

"Iron Bender!" exploded Gentle Maiden. "That lump! That obstinate, leatherheaded strap-cutter! That—"

"Come to think of it, Gentle," interrupted the Hill Bluffer, "how come Iron Bender isn't here? I'd have thought you'd have brought him along instead of these imitation Grandfathers—"

"There, now," sighed One Punch, staring off at the mountains beyond the other side of the valley. "That bit about imitations— That's just the sort of remark I might've taken a bit of offense at, back in the days before I developed wisdom. But does it trouble me nowdays?"

"No offense meant, One Punch," said the Bluffer. "You know I didn't meant that."

"None taken. You see, Granddaughter?" said One Punch. "The postman here never meant a bit of offense; and in the old days I wouldn't have seen it until it was too late."

"Oh, you make me sick!" blazed Gentle Maiden. "You all make me sick. Iron Bender makes me sick, saying he won't have anything against this Law-Twister Shorty until the Law-Twister tries twisting the Clan law that says those three poor little orphans belong to me now!" She glared at the Bluffer and Mal. "Iron Bender said the Shorty can come find him, any time he really wanted to, down at the harness shop!"

"He'll be right down," promised the Bluffer.

"Hey—" began Mal. But nobody was paying any attention to him.

"Now, Granddaughter," One Punch was saying, reprovingly. "The Bender didn't exactly ask you to name him your protector, you know."

"What difference does that make?" snapped Gentle Maiden. "I had to pick the toughest man in the Clan to protect me—that's just common sense; even if he *is* stubborn as an I-don't-know-what and thick-headed as a log wall! I know my rights. He's got to defend me; and there—" she wheeled and pointed to the large boulder lying on the grass, "—there's the stone of Mighty Grappler, and here's all three of you, one of who's got to be a Grandfather by next Clan meeting—and you mean to tell me none of you'll even say a word to help me turn this postman and this Shorty around and get them out of here?"

The three elderly Dilbian males looked back at her without speaking.

"All right!" roared Gentle Maiden, stamping about to turn her back on all of them. "You'll be sorry! All of you!"

With that, she marched off down the slope of the valley toward the village of log houses.

"Well," said the individual whom the Hill Bluffer had

called Grandpa Tricky, "guess that's that, until she thinks up something more. I might as well be ambling back down to the house, myself. How about you, Forty Winks?"

"Guess I might as well, too," said Forty Winks.

They went off after Gentle Maiden, leaving Mal—still on the Hill Bluffer's back—staring down at One Punch, from just behind the Bluffer's reddish-furred right ear.

"What," asked Mal, "has the stone of what's-his-name got to do with it?"

"The stone of Mighty Grappler?" asked One Punch. "You mean you don't know about that stone, over there?"

"Law-Twister here's just a Shorty," said the Bluffer, apologetically. "You know how Shorties are—tough, but pretty ignorant."

"Some *say* they're tough," said One Punch, squinting up at Mal, speculatively.

"Now, wait a minute, One Punch!" the Hill Bluffer's bass voice dropped ominously an additional half-octave. "Maybe there's something we ought to get straight right now! This isn't just any plain private citizen you're talking to, it's the official postman speaking. And *I* say Shorties're tough. *I* say I was there when the Half-Pint Posted took the Streamside Terror; and also when Pick-and-Shovel wiped up Bone Breaker in a sword-and-shield duel. Now, no disrespect, but if you're questioning the official word of a government mail carrier—"

"Now, Bluffer," said One Punch, "I never doubted you personally for a minute. It's just everybody knows the Terror and Bone Breaker weren't either of them pushovers. But you know I'm not the biggest man around, by a long shot; and now and then during my time I can remember laying out some pretty good-sized scrappers, myself—when my temper got away from me, that is. So I know from personal experience not every man's as tough as the next—and why shouldn't that work for Shorties as well as real men? Maybe those two you carried before were tough; but how can anybody tell about this Shorty? No offense, up there, Law-Twister, by the way. Just using a bit of my wisdom and asking."

Mal opened his mouth and shut it again.

"Well?" growled the Bluffer underneath him. "Speak up, Law-Twister." Suddenly, there was a dangerous feeling of tension in the air. Mal swallowed. How, he thought, would a Dilbian answer a question like that?

Any way but with a straight answer, came back the reply from the hypnotrained section of his mind.

"Well—er," said Mal, "how can I tell you how tough I am? I mean, what's tough by the standards of you real men? As far as we Shorties go, it might be one thing. For you real men, it might be something else completely. It's too bad I didn't ever know this Half-Pint Posted, or Pick-and-Shovel, or else I could kind of measure myself by them for you. But I never heard of them until now."

"But you think they just *might* be tougher than you, though—the Half-Pint and Pick-and-Shovel?" demanded One Punch.

"Oh, sure," said Mal. "They could both be ten times as tough as I am. And then, again— Well, not for me to say."

There was a moment's silence from both the Dilbians, then the Bluffer broke it with a snort of admiration.

"Hor!" he chortled admiringly to One Punch. "I guess you can see now how the Law-Twister here got his name. Slippery? Slippery's not the word for this Shorty."

But One Punch shook his head.

"Slippery's one thing," he said. "But law-twisting's another. Here he says he doesn't even know about the stone of Mighty Grappler. How's he going to go about twisting laws if he doesn't know about the laws in the first place?"

"You could tell me about the stone," suggested Mal.

"Mighty Grappler put it there, Law-Twister," said the Bluffer. "Set it up to keep peace in Clan Water Gap."

"Better let me tell him, Postman," interrupted One Punch. "After all, he ought to get it straight from a born Water Gapper. Look at the stone there, Law-Twister. You see those two ends of iron sticking out of it?"

Mal looked. Sure enough, there were two lengths of rusty metal protruding from opposite sides of the boulder, which was about three feet in width in the middle.

"I see them," he answered.

"Mighty Grappler was just maybe the biggest and strongest real man who ever lived—"

The Hill Bluffer coughed.

"One Man, now . . ." he murmured.

"I'm not denying One Man's something like a couple of big men in one skin, Postman," said One Punch. "But the stories about Mighty Grappler are hard to beat. He was a stonemason, Law-Twister; and he founded Clan Water Gap, with himself, his relatives, and his descendants. Now, as long as he was alive, there was no trouble. He was Clan Water Gap's first Grandfather, and even when he was a hundred and ten nobody wanted to argue with him. But he worried about keeping things orderly after he was gone—"

"Fell off a cliff at a hundred and fourteen," put in the Bluffer. "Broke his neck. Otherwise, no telling how long he'd have lived."

"Excuse me, Postman," said One Punch. "But I'm telling

this, not you. The point is, Law-Twister, he was worried like I say about keeping the Clan orderly. So he took a stone he was working on one day—that stone there, that no one but him could come near lifting—and hammered an iron rod through it to make a handhold on each side, like you see. Then he picked the stone up, carried it here, and set it down; and he made a law. The rules he'd made earlier for Clan Water Gappers were to stand as laws, themselves—as long as that stone stayed where it was. But if anyone ever came along who could pick it up all by himself and carry it as much as ten steps, then that was a sign it was time the laws should change."

Mal stared at the boulder. His hypnotraining had informed him that while Dilbians would go to any lengths to twist the truth to their own advantage, the one thing they would not stand for, in themselves or others, was an out-and-out lie. Accordingly, One Punch would probably be telling the truth about this Mighty Grappler ancestor of his. On the other hand, a chunk of granite that size must weigh at least a ton—maybe a ton and a half. Not even an outsize Dilbian could be imagined carrying something like that for ten paces. There were natural flesh-and-blood limits, even for these giant natives—or were there?

"Did anybody ever try lifting it, after that?" Mal asked.

"Hor!" snorted the Bluffer.

"Now, Law-Twister," said One Punch, almost reproachfully, "any Clan Water Gapper's got too much sense to make a fool of himself trying to do something only the Mighty Grappler had a chance of doing. That stone's never been touched from that day to this—and that's the way it should be."

"I suppose so," said Mal.

The Bluffer snorted again, in surprise. One Punch stared.

"You giving up—just like that, Law-Twister?" demanded the Bluffer.

"What? I don't understand," said Mal, confused. "We were just talking about the stone—"

"But you said you supposed that's the way it should be," said the Bluffer, outraged. "The stone there, and the laws just the way Mighty Grappler laid them down. What kind of a law-twister are you, anyway?"

"But . . ." Mal was still confused. "What's the Mighty Grappler and his stone got to do with my getting back these three Shorties that Gentle Maiden says she adopted?"

"Why, that's one of Mighty Grappler's laws—one of the ones he made and backed up with the stone!" said One Punch. "It was Mighty Grappler said that any orphans running around loose could be adopted by any single woman of the Clan, who could then name herself a protector to take care of them and her! Now, that's Clan law."

"But—" began Mal again. He had not expected to have to start arguing his case this soon. But it seemed there was no choice. "It's Clan law if you say so; and I don't have any quarrel with it. But these people Gentle Maiden's adopted aren't orphans. They're Shorties. That's why she's going to have to let them go."

"So that's the way you twist it," said One Punch, almost in a tone of satisfaction. "Figured you'd come up with something like that. So, you say they're not orphans?"

"Of course, that's what I say!" said Mal.

"Figured as much. Naturally, Gentle says they are."

"Well, I'll just have to make her understand—"

"Not her," interrupted the Bluffer.

"Naturally not her," said One Punch. "If *she* says they're

orphans, then its her protector you've got to straighten things out with. Gentle says 'orphans,' so Iron Bender's going to be saying 'orphans,' too. You and Iron Bender got to get together."

"And none of that sissy lowland stuff with swords and shields," put in the Hill Bluffer. "Just honest, man-to-man, teeth, claws, and muscle. You don't have to worry about Iron Bender going in for any of that modern stuff, Law-Twister."

"Oh?" said Mal, staring.

"Thought I'd tell you right now," said the Bluffer. "Ease your mind, in case you were wondering."

"I wasn't, actually," said Mal, numbly, still trying to make his mind believe what his ears seemed to be hearing.

"Well," said One Punch, "how about it, Postman? Law-Twister? Shall we get on down to the harness shop and you and Iron Bender can set up the details? Quite a few folks been dropping in the last few hours to see the two of you tangle. Don't think any of them ever saw a Shorty in action before. Know I never did myself. Should be real interesting."

He and the Hill Bluffer had already turned and begun to stroll down toward the village.

"Interesting's not the word for it," the Bluffer responded. "Seen it twice, myself, and I can tell you it's a sight to behold. . . ."

He continued along, chatting cheerfully while Mal rode along helplessly on Dilbian-back, his head spinning. The log buildings got closer and closer.

"Wait—" Mal said desperately, as they entered the street running down the center of the cluster of log structures.

The Bluffer and One Punch both stopped. One Punch turned to gaze up at him.

"Wait?" One Punch said. "What for?"

"I—I can't," stammered Mal, frantically searching for an excuse, and going on talking meanwhile with the first words that came to his lips. "That is, I've got my own laws to think of. Shorty laws. Responsibilities. I can't just go representing these other Shorty orphans just like that. I have to be . . . uh, briefed."

"Briefed?" The Bluffer's tongue struggled with pronunciation of the human word Mal had used.

"Yes—uh, that means I have to be given authority—like Gentle Maiden had to choose Iron Bender as her protector," said Mal. "These Shorty orphans have to agree to choose me as their law-twister. It's one of the Shorty freedoms—freedom to not be defended by a law-twister without your consent. With so much at stake here—I mean, not just what might happen to me, or Iron Bender, but what might happen to Clan Water Gap laws or Shorty laws—I need to consult with my clients, I mean these other Shorties I'm working for, before I enter into any—er—discussion with Gentle Maiden's protector."

Mal stopped speaking and waited, his heart hammering away. There was a moment of deep silence from both the Bluffer and One Punch. Then One Punch spoke to the taller Dilbian.

"Have to admit you're right, Postman," One Punch said, admiringly. "He sure can twist. You understand all that he was talking about, there?"

"Why, of course," said the Bluffer. "After all, I've had a lot to do with these Shorties. He was saying that this isn't just any little old hole-and-corner tangle between him and Iron Bender—this is a high-class hassle to decide the law; and it's got to be done right. No offense, One Punch, but you, having been in the habit of getting right down to business on the spur of the moment all those years, might not have stopped to think just how important it is not to rush matters in an important case like this."

"No offense taken, Postman," said One Punch, easily. "Though I must say maybe it's lucky you didn't know me in my younger, less full-of-wisdom days. Because it seems to me we were *both* maybe about to rush the Law-Twister a mite."

"Well, now," said the Bluffer. "Leaving aside that business of my luck and all that about not knowing you when you were younger, I guess I have to admit perhaps I *was* a little on the rushing side, myself. Anyway, Law-Twister's straightened us both out. So, what's the next thing you want to do, Law-Twister?"

"Well . . ." said Mal. He was still thinking desperately. "This being a matter that concerns the laws governing the whole Water Gap Clan, as well as Shorty laws and the stone of Mighty Grappler, we probably ought to get everyone together. I mean we ought to talk it over. It might well turn out to be this is something that ought to be settled not by a fight but in—"

Mal had not expected the Dilbians to have a word for it; but he was wrong. His hypnotraining threw the proper Dilbian sounds up for his tongue to utter.

"—court," he wound up.

"Court? Can't have a court, Law-Twister," said One Punch. He and the Hill Bluffer had stopped in the middle of the village street when Mal started talking. Now a small crowd of the local Dilbians was gathering around them, listening to the conversation.

"Thought you knew that, Law-Twister," put in the Bluffer, reprovingly. "Can't have a Clan court without a Grandfather to decide things."

"Too bad, in a way," said One Punch with a sigh. "We'd all like to see a real Law-Twister Shorty at work in a real court situation, twisting and slickering around from one argument to the next. But, just as the Bluffer says, Twister, we've got no Grandfather yet. Won't have until the next Clan meeting."

"When's that?" asked Mal, hastily.

"Couple of weeks," said One Punch. "Be glad to wait around a couple of weeks far as all of us here're concerned; but those Shorty orphans of Gentle Maiden's are getting pretty hungry and even a mite thirsty. Seems they won't eat anything she gives them; and they even don't seem to like to drink the well water, much. Gentle figures they won't settle down until they get it straight that they're adopted and not going home again. So she wants you and Iron Bender to settle it right now—and, of course, since she's a member of the Clan, the Clan backs her up on that."

"Won't eat or drink? Where are they?" asked Mal.

"At Gentle's house," said One Punch. "She's got them locked up there so they can't run back to that box they came down in and fly away back into the sky. Real motherly instincts in that girl, if I do say so myself who's her real grandpa. That, and looks, too. Can't understand why no young buck's snapped her up before this—"

"You understand, all right, One Punch," interrupted an incredibly deep bass voice; and there shouldered through the crowd a darkly brown-haired Dilbian, taller than any of the crowd around him. The speaker was shorter by half a head than the Hill Bluffer—the postman seemed to have the advantage in height on every other native Mal had seen —but this newcomer towered over everyone else and he was a walking mass of muscle, easily outweighing the Bluffer.

"You understand, all right," he repeated, stopping before the Bluffer and Mal. "Folks'd laugh their heads off at any man who'd offer to take a girl as tough-minded as Gentle, to wife—that is, unless he had to. Then, maybe he'd find it was worth it. But do it on his own? Pride's pride. . . . Hello there, Postman. This the Law-Twister Shorty?"

"It's him," said the Bluffer.

"Why he's no bigger'n those other little Shorties," said the deep-voiced Dilbian, peering over the Bluffer's shoulder at Mal.

"You go thinking size is all there is to a Shorty, you're going to be surprised," said the Bluffer. "Along with the Streamside Terror and Bone Breaker, as I recollect. Twister, this here's Gentle's protector and the Clan Water Gap harnessmaker, Iron Bender."

"Uh—pleased to meet you," said Mal.

"Pleased to meet you, Law-Twister," rumbled Iron Bender. "That is, I'm pleased now; and I hope I go on being pleased. I'm a plain, simple man, Law-Twister. A good day's work, a good night's sleep, four good meals a day, and I'm satisfied. You wouldn't find me mixed up in fancy doings like this by choice. I'd have nothing to do with this if Gentle hadn't named me her protector. But right's right. She did; and I am, like it or not."

"I know how you feel," said Mal, hastily. "I was actually going someplace else when the Shorties here had me come see about this situation. I hadn't planned on it at all."

"Well, well," said Iron Bender, deeply, "you, too, eh?" He sighed heavily.

"That's the way things go, nowdays, though," he said. "A plain simple man can't hardly do a day's work in peace without some maiden or someone coming to him for protection. So they got you, too, eh? Well, well—life's life, and a man can't do much about it. You're not a bad little Shorty at all. I'm going to be real sorry to tear your head off—which of course I'm going to do, since I figure I probably could have done the same to Bone Breaker or the Streamside Terror, if it'd ever happened to come to that. Not that I'm a boastful man; but true's true."

He sighed again.

"So," he said, flexing his huge arms, "if you'll just light down from your perch on the postman, there, I'll get to it. I've got a long day's work back at the harness shop, anyway; and daylight's daylight—"

"But fair's fair," broke in Mal, hastily. The Iron Bender lowered his massive, brown-furred hands, looking puzzled.

"Fair's fair?" he echoed.

"You heard him, harnessmaker!" snapped the Bluffer, bristling. "No offense, but there's more to something like this than punching holes in leather. Nothing I'd like to see more than for you to try—just try—to tear the head off a Shorty like Law-Twister here, since I've seen what a Shorty can do when he really gets his dander up. But like the Twister himself pointed out, this is not just a happy hassle—this is serious business involving Clan laws and Shorty laws and lots of other things. We were just discussing it when you came up. Law-Twister was saying maybe something like this should be held up until the next Clan meeting when you elect a Grandfather, so's it could be decided by a legal Clan Water Gap court in full session."

"Court—" Iron Bender was beginning when he was interrupted.

"We will *not* wait for any court to settle who gets my orphans!" cried a new voice and the black-furred form of Gentle Maiden shoved through the crowd to join them. "When there's no Clan Grandfather to rule, the Clan goes by law and custom. Law and custom says my protector's got to take care of me, and I've got to take care of the little ones I adopted. And I'm not letting them suffer for two weeks before they realize they're settling down with me. The law says I don't have to and no man's going to make me try—"

"Now, hold on there just a minute, Gentle," rumbled Iron Bender. "Guess maybe I'm the one man in this Clan, or between here and Humrog Peak for that matter, who could make you try and do something whether you wanted it or not, if he wanted to. Not that I'm saying I'm going to, now. But you just remember that while I'm your named protector, it doesn't mean I'm going to let you order me around like you do other folk—any more than I ever did."

He turned back to the Bluffer, Mal, and One Punch.

"Right's right," he said. "Now, what's all this about a court?"

Neither the Bluffer nor One Punch answered immediately—and, abruptly, Mal realized it was up to him to do the explaining.

"Well, as I was pointing out to the postman and One Punch," he began, rapidly, "there's a lot at stake, here. I mean, we Shorties have laws, too; and one of them is that you don't have to be represented by a law-twister not your choice. I haven't talked to these Shorties you and Gentle claim are orphans, so I don't have their word on going ahead with anything on their behalf. I can't do anything important until I have that word of theirs. What if we—er—tangled, and it turned out they didn't mean to name me to do anything for them, after all? Here you, a regular named protector of a maiden according to your Clan laws, as laid down by Mighty Grappler, would have been hassling with someone who didn't have a shred of right to fight you. And here, too, I'd have been tangling without a shred of lawful reason for it, to back me up. What we need to do is study the situation. I need to talk to the Shorties you say are orphans—"

"No!" cried Gentle Maiden. "He's not to come *near* my little orphans and get them all upset, even more than they are now—"

"Hold on, now, Granddaughter," interposed One Punch. "We all can see how the Twister here's twisting and slipping around like the clever little Shorty he is, trying to get things his way. But he's got a point there when he talks about Clan Water Gap putting up a named protector, and then that protector turns out to have gotten into a hassle with someone with no authority at all. Why they'd be laughing at our Clan all up and down the mountains. Worse yet, what if that protector should lose—"

"*Lose?*" snorted Iron Bender, with all the geniality of a grizzly abruptly wakened from his long winter's nap.

"That's right, harnessmaker. *Lose!*" snarled the Hill Bluffer. "Guess there just might be a real man not too far away from you at this moment who's pretty sure you *would* lose—and handily!"

Suddenly, the two of them were standing nose to nose. Mal became abruptly aware that he was still seated in the saddle arrangement on the Bluffer's back and that, in case of trouble between the two big Dilbians, it would not be easy for him to get down in a hurry.

"I'll tell you what, Postman," Iron Bender was growling. "Why don't you and I just step out beyond the houses, here, where there's a little more open space—"

"Stop it!" snapped Gentle Maiden. "Stop it right now, Iron Bender! You've got no right to go fighting anybody for your own private pleasure when you're still my protector. What if something happened, and you weren't able to protect me and mine the way you should after that?"

"Maiden's right," said One Punch, sharply. "It's Clan honor and decency at stake here; not just your own feelings, Bender. Now, as I was saying, Law-Twister here's been doing some fine talking and twisting, and he's come up with a real point. It's as much a matter to us if he's a real Shorty-type protector to those orphans Maiden adopted, as it is to him and the other Shorties—"

His voice became mild. He turned to the crowd and spread his hands, modestly.

"Of course, I'm no real Grandfather," he said. "Some might think I wouldn't stand a chance to be the one you'll pick at that next Clan meeting. Of course, some might think I would, too—but it's hardly for me to say. Only, speaking as a man who *might* be named a Grandfather someday, I'd say Gentle Maiden really ought to let Law-Twister check with those three orphans to see if they want him to talk or hassle, for them."

A bass-voiced murmur of agreement rose from the surrounding crowd, which by this time had grown to a respectable size.

For the first time since he had said farewell to Ambassador Joshua Guy, Mal felt his spirits begin to rise. For the first time, he seemed to be getting some control over the events which had been hurrying him along like a chip swirling downstream in the current of a fast river. Maybe, if he had a little luck, now—

"Duty's duty, I guess," rumbled Iron Bender at just this moment. "All right then, Law-Twister—now, stop your arguing, Gentle, it's no use—you can see your fellow Shorties. They're at Gentle's place, last but one on the left-hand side of the street, here."

"Show you the way, myself, Postman," said One Punch.

The Clan elder led off, limping, and the crowd broke up as the Hill Bluffer followed him. Iron Bender went off in the opposite direction, but Gentle Maiden tagged along with the postman, Mal, and her grandfather, muttering to herself.

"Take things kind of hard, don't you, Gentle?" said the Hill Bluffer to her, affably. "Don't blame old Iron Bender. Man can't expect to win every time."

"Why not?" demanded Gentle. "I do! He's just so cautious, and slow, he makes me sick! Why can't he be like One Punch, here, when *he* was young? Hit first and think afterward—particularly when I ask him to? Then Bender could go around being slow and careful about his own business if he wanted; in fact, I'd be all for him being like that, on his own time. A girl needs a man she can respect; particularly when there's no other man around that's much more than half-size to him!"

"Tell him so," suggested the Bluffer, strolling along, his long legs making a single stride to each two of Gentle and One Punch.

"Certainly not! It'd look like I was giving in to him!" said Gentle. "It may be all right for any old ordinary girl to go chasing a man, but not me. Folks know me better than that. They'd laugh their heads off if I suddenly started going all soft on Bender. And besides—"

"Here we are, Postman—Law-Twister," interrupted One Punch, stopping by the heavy wooden door of a good-sized log building. "This is Gentle's place. The orphans are inside."

"Don't you go letting them out, now!" snapped Gentle, as Mal, relieved to be out of the saddle after this much time in it, began sliding down the Bluffer's broad back toward the ground.

"Don't worry, Granddaughter," said One Punch, as Mal's boots touched the earth. "Postman and I'll wait right outside the door here with you. If one of them tries to duck out, we'll catch him or her for you."

"They keep wanting to go back to their flying box," said Gentle. "And I know the minute one of them gets inside it, he'll be into the air and off like a flash. I haven't gone to all this trouble to lose any of them, now. So, don't you try anything while you're inside there, Law-Twister!"

Mal went up the three wooden steps to the rough plank door and lifted a latch that was, from the standpoint of a human-sized individual, like a heavy bar locking the door shut. The door yawned open before him, and he stepped through into dimness. The door swung shut behind him, and he heard the latch being relocked.

"Holler when you want out, Law-Twister!" One Punch's voice boomed through the closed door. Mal looked around him.

He was in what was obviously a Dilbian home. A few pieces of heavy, oversize furniture supplemented a long plank table before an open fireplace, in which, however, no fire was now burning. Two more doors, also latched, were of rooms beyond this one.

He crossed the room and tried the right-hand door at random. It gave him a view of an empty, kitchenlike room with what looked like a side of beef hanging from a hook in a far corner. A chopping block and a wash trough of hollowed-out stone furnished the rest of the room.

Mal backed out, closed the door, and tried the one on his left. It opened easily, but the entrance to the room beyond was barred by a rough fence of planks some eight feet high, with sharp chips of stone hammered into the tops. Through the gap in the planks, Mal looked into what seemed a large Dilbian bed chamber, which had been converted into human living quarters by the simple expedient of ripping out three cabin sections from a shuttle boat and setting them up like so many large tin boxes on the floor under the lofty, log-beamed roof.

At the sound of the opening of the door, other doors opened in the transplanted cabin sections. As Mal watched, three middle-aged people—one woman and two men—emerged each from his own cabin and stopped short to stare through the gaps in the plank fence at him.

"Oh, no!" said one of the men, a skinny, balding character with a torn shirt collar. "A kid!"

"Kid?" echoed Mal, grimly. He had been prepared to feel

sorry for the three captives of Gentle Maiden, but this kind of reception did not make it easy. "How adult do you have to be to wrestle a Dilbian?"

"Wrestle . . . !" It was the woman. She stared at him. "Oh, it surely won't come to that. Will it? You ought to be able to find a way around it. Didn't they pick you because you'd be able to understand these natives?"

Mal looked at her narrowly.

"How would you have any idea of how I was picked?" he asked.

"We just assumed they'd send someone to help us who understood these natives," she said.

Mal's conscience pricked him.

"I'm sorry—er—Mrs. . . ." he began.

"Ora Page," she answered. "This—" she indicated the thin man, "is Harvey Anok, and—" she nodded at the other, "Zora Rice." She had a soft, rather gentle face, in contrast to the sharp, almost suspicious face of the Harvey Anok and the rather hard features of Zora Rice; but like both of the others, she had a tanned outdoors sort of look.

"Mrs. Page," Mal said. "I'm sorry, but the only thing I seem to be able to do for you is get myself killed by the local harnessmaker. But I do have an idea. Where's this shuttle boat you came down in?"

"Right behind this building we're in," said Harvey, "in a meadow about a hundred yards back. What about it?"

"Good," said Mal. "I'm going to try to make a break for it. Now, if you can just tell me how to take off in it, and land, I think I can fly it. I'll make some excuse to get inside it and get into the air. Then I'll fly back to the ambassador who sent me out here, and tell him I can't do anything.

He'll have to send in force, if necessary, to get you out of this."

The three stared back at him without speaking.

"Well?" demanded Mal. "What about it? If I get killed by that harnessmaker it's not going to do you any good. Gentle Maiden may decide to take you away and hide you someplace in the mountains, and no rescue team will ever find you. What're you waiting for? Tell me how to fly that shuttle boat!"

The three of them looked at each other uncomfortably and then back at Mal. Harvey shook his head.

"No," he said. "I don't think we ought to do that. There's a treaty—"

"The Human-Hemnoid Treaty on this planet?" Mal asked. "But, I just told you, that Dilbian harnessmaker may kill me. You might be killed, too. Isn't it more important to save lives than worry about a treaty at a time like this?"

"You don't understand," said Harvey. "One of the things that Treaty particularly rules out is anthropologists. If we're found here—"

"But I thought you were tourists?" Mal said.

"We are. All of us were on vacation on a spaceliner tour. It just happens we three are anthropologists, too—"

"That's why we were tempted to drop in here in the first place," put in Zora Rice.

"But that Treaty's a lot more important than you think," Harvey said. "We can't risk damaging it."

"Why didn't you think of that before you came here?" Mal growled.

"You can find a way out for all of us without calling for armed force and getting us all in trouble. I know you can," said Ora Page. "We trust you. Won't you try?"

Mal stared back at them all, scowling. There was something funny about all this. Prisoners who hadn't worried about a Human-Hemnoid Treaty on their way to Dilbia, but who were willing to risk themselves to protect it now that they were here. A Dilbian female who wanted to adopt three full-grown humans. Why, in the name of all that was sensible? A village harnessmaker ready to tear him apart, and a human ambassador who had sent him blithely out to face that same harnessmaker with neither advice nor protection.

"All right," said Mal, grimly. "I'll talk to you again later—with luck."

He stepped back and swung closed the heavy door to the room in which they were fenced. Going to the entrance of the building, he shouted to One Punch, and the door before him was opened from the outside. Gentle Maiden shouldered suspiciously past him into the house as he emerged.

"Well, how about it, Law-Twister?" asked One Punch, as the door closed behind Gentle Maiden. "Those other Shorties say it was all right for you to talk and hassle for them?"

"Well, yes . . ." said Mal. He gazed narrowly up into the large furry faces of One Punch and the Bluffer, trying to read their expressions. But outside of the fact that they both looked genial, he could discover nothing. The alien visages held their secrets well from human eyes.

"They agreed, all right," said Mal, slowly. "But what they had to say to me sort of got me thinking. Maybe you can tell me—just why is it Clan Water Gap can't hold its meeting right away instead of two weeks from now? Hold a meeting right now and the Clan could have an elected Grandfather before the afternoon's half over. Then there'd be time to hold a regular Clan court, for example, between the election and sunset; and this whole matter of the orphan Shorties could be handled more in regular fashion."

"Wondered that, did you, Law-Twister?" said One Punch. "It just crossed my mind earlier you might wonder about it. No real reason why the Clan meeting couldn't be held right away, I guess. Only, who's going to suggest it?"

"Suggest it?" Mal said.

"Why, sure," said One Punch. "Ordinarily, when a Clan has a Grandfather, it'd be up to the Grandfather to suggest it. But Clan Water Gap doesn't have a Grandfather right now, as you know."

"Isn't there anyone else to suggest things like that if a Grandfather isn't available?" asked Mal.

"Well, yes." One Punch gazed thoughtfully away from Mal, down the village street. "If there's no Grandfather around, it'd be pretty much up to one of the grandpas to suggest it. Only—of course I can't speak for old Forty Winks or anyone else—but I wouldn't want to be the one to do it, myself. Might sound like I thought I had a better chance of being elected Grandfather now, than I would two weeks from now."

"So," said Mal. "You won't suggest it, and if you won't I can see how the others wouldn't, for the same reason. Who else does that leave who might suggest it?"

"Why, I don't know, Law-Twister," said One Punch, gazing back at him. "Guess any strong-minded member of the Clan could speak up and propose it. Someone like Gentle Maiden, herself, for example. But you know Gentle Maiden isn't about to suggest anything like that when what she wants is for Iron Bender to try and take you apart as soon as possible."

"How about Iron Bender?" Mal asked.

"Now, he just might want to suggest something like that," said One Punch, "being how as he likes to do everything just right. But it might look like he was trying to get out of tangling with you—after all this talk by the Bluffer, here, about how tough Shorties are. So I don't expect Bender'd be likely to say anything about changing the meeting time."

Mal looked at the tall Dilbian who had brought him here. "Bluffer," he said, "I wonder if you—"

"Look here, Law-Twister," said the Hill Bluffer severely. "I'm the government postman—to all the Clans and towns and folks from Wildwood Valley to Humrog Peak. A government man like myself can't go sticking his nose into local affairs."

"But you were ready to tangle with Iron Bender yourself, a little while ago—"

"That was personal and private. This is public. I don't blame you for not seeing the difference right off, Law-Twister, you being a Shorty and all," said the Bluffer, "but a government man has to know, and keep the two things separate."

He fell silent, looking at Mal. For a moment neither the Bluffer nor One Punch said anything; but Mal was left with the curious feeling that the conversation had not so much been ended, as left hanging in the air for him to pick up. He was beginning to get an understanding of how Dilbian minds worked. Because of their taboo against any outright lying, they were experts at pretending to say one thing while actually saying another. There was a strong notion in Mal's mind now that somehow the other two were simply waiting for him to ask the right question—as if he had a handful of keys and only the right one would unlock an answer with the information he wanted.

"Certainly is different from the old days, Postman," said One Punch, idly, turning to the Bluffer. "Wonder what Mighty Grappler would have said, seeing Shorties like the Law-Twister among us. He'd have said something, all right. Had an answer for everything, Mighty Grappler did."

An idea exploded into life in Mal's mind. Of course! That was it!

"Isn't there something in Mighty Grappler's laws," he asked, "that could arrange for a Clan meeting without someone suggesting it?"

One Punch looked back at him.

"Why, what do you know?" the oldster said. "Bluffer, Law-Twister here is something to make up stories about, all right. Imagine a Shorty guessing that Mighty Grappler had thought of something like that, when I'd almost forgotten it myself."

"Shorties are sneaky little characters, as I've said before," replied the Bluffer, gazing down at Mal with obvious pride. "Quick on the uptake, too."

"Then there is a way?" Mal asked.

"It just now comes back to me," said One Punch. "Mighty Grappler set up all his laws to protect the Clan members against themselves and each other and against strangers. But he did make one law to protect strangers on Clan territory. As I remember, any stranger having a need to appeal to the whole Clan for justice was supposed to stand beside Grappler's stone—the one we showed you on the way in—and put his hand on it, and make that appeal."

"Then what?" asked Mal. "The Clan would grant his appeal?"

"Well, not exactly," said One Punch. "But they'd be obliged to talk the matter over and decide things."

"Oh," said Mal. This was less than he had hoped for, but still he had a strong feeling now that he was on the right track. "Well, let's go."

"Right," said the Bluffer. He and One Punch turned and strolled off up the street.

"Hey!" yelled Mal, trotting after them. The Bluffer turned around, picked him up, and stuffed him into the saddle on the postman's back.

"Sorry, Law-Twister. Forgot about those short legs of yours," the Bluffer said. Turning to stroll forward with One Punch again, he added to the oldster, "Makes you kind of wonder how they made out to start off with, before they had flying boxes and things like that."

"Probably didn't do much," offered One Punch in explanation, "just lay in the sun and dug little burrows and things like that."

Mal opened his mouth and then closed it again on the first retort that had come to his lips.

"Where you off to with the Law-Twister now, One Punch?" asked a graying-haired Dilbian they passed, whom Mal was pretty sure was either Forty Winks or Grandpa Tricky.

"Law-Twister's going up to the stone of Mighty Grappler to make an appeal to the Clan," said One Punch.

"Well, now," said the other, "guess I'll mosey up there myself and have a look at that. Can't remember it ever happening before."

He fell in behind them, but halfway down the street fell

out again to answer the questions of several other bystanders who wanted to know what was going on. So it was that when Mal alighted from the Bluffer's back at the stone of Mighty Grappler, there was just he and the Bluffer and One Punch there, although a few figures could be seen beginning to stream out of the village toward the stone.

"Go ahead, Law-Twister," said One Punch, nodding at the stone. "Make that appeal of yours."

"Hadn't I better wait until the rest of the Clan gets here?"

"I suppose you could do that," said One Punch. "I was thinking you might just want to say your appeal and have it over with and sort of let me tell people about it. But you're right. Wait until folks get here. Give you a chance to kind of look over Mighty Grappler's stone, too, and put yourself in the kind of spirit to make a good appeal. . . . Guess you'll want to be remembering this word for word, to pass on down the line to the other clans, won't you, Postman?"

"You could say I've almost a duty to do that, One Punch," responded the Bluffer. "Lots more to being a government postman than some people think. . . ."

The two went on chatting, turning a little away from Mal and the stone to gaze down the slope at the Clan members on their way up from the village. Mal turned to gaze at the stone, itself. It was still inconceivable to him that even a Dilbian could lift and carry such a weight ten paces.

Certainly, it did not look as if anyone had ever moved the stone since it had been placed here. The two ends of the iron rod sticking out from opposite sides of it were red with rust, and the grass had grown up thickly around its base. That is, it had grown up thickly everywhere but just behind it, where it looked like a handful of grass might have been pulled up, recently. Bending down to look closer at the grass-free part of the stone, Mal caught sight of something dark. The edge of some indentation, almost something like the edge of a large hole in the stone itself—

"Law-Twister!" The voice of One Punch brought Mal abruptly upright. He saw that the vanguard of the Dilbians coming out of the village was almost upon them.

"How'd you like me to sort of pass the word what this is all about?" asked One Punch. "Then you could just make your appeal without trying to explain it?"

"Oh—fine," said Mal. He glanced back at the stone. For a moment he felt a great temptation to take hold of the two rust-red iron handles and see if he actually could lift it. But there were too many eyes on him now.

The members of the Clan came up and sat down, with their backs straight and furry legs stuck out before them on the grass. The Bluffer, however, remained standing near Mal, as did One Punch. Among the last to arrive was Gentle Maiden, who hurried up to the very front of the crowd and snorted angrily at Mal before sitting down.

"Got them all upset!" she said, triumphantly. "Knew you would!"

Iron Bender had not put in an appearance.

"Members of Clan Water Gap," said One Punch, when they were all settled on the grass and quiet, "you all know what this Shorty, Law-Twister here, dropped in on us to do. He wants to take back with him the orphans Gentle Maiden adopted according to Clan law, as laid down by Mighty Grappler. Naturally, Maiden doesn't want him to, and she's got her protector, Iron Bender—"

He broke off, peering out over the crowd.

"Where is Iron Bender?" the oldster demanded.

"He says work's work," a voice answered from the crowd. "Says to send somebody for him when you're all ready to have someone's head torn off. Otherwise, he'll be busy down in the harness shop."

Gentle Maiden snorted.

"Well, well. I guess we'll just have to go on without him," said One Punch. "As I was saying, here's Iron Bender all ready to do his duty; but as Law-Twister sees it, it's not all that simple."

There was a buzz of low-toned, admiring comments from the crowd. One Punch waited until the noise died before going on.

"One thing Law-Twister wants to do is make an appeal to the Clan, according to Mighty Grappler's law, before he gets down to tangling with Iron Bender," the oldster said. "So, without my bending your ears any further, here's the Law-Twister himself, with tongue all oiled up and ready to talk you upside down, and roundabout— Go ahead, Law-Twister!"

Mal put his hand on the stone of Mighty Grappler. In fact, he leaned on the stone and it seemed to him it rocked a little bit, under his weight. It did not seem to him that One Punch's introductory speech had struck quite the serious note Mal himself might have liked. But now, in any case, it was up to him.

"Uh—members of Clan Water Gap," he said. "I've been disturbed by a lot of what I've learned here. For example, here you have something very important at stake—the right of a Clan Water Gap maiden to adopt Shorties as orphans. But the whole matter has to be settled by what's really an emergency measure—that is, my tangling with Iron Bender —just because Clan Water Gap hasn't elected a new Grandfather lately, and the meeting to elect one is a couple of weeks away—"

"And while it's not for me to say," interrupted the basso voice of the Hill Bluffer, "not being a Clan Water Gapper myself, and besides being a government postman who's strictly not concerned in any local affairs—I'd guess that's what a lot of folks are going to be asking me as I ply my route between here and Humrog Peak in the next few weeks. 'How come they didn't hold a regular trial to settle the matter, down there in Clan Water Gap?' they'll be asking. 'Because they didn't have a Grandfather,' I'll have to say. 'How come those Water Gappers are running around without a Grandfather?' they'll ask—"

"All right, Postman!" interrupted One Punch, in his turn. "I guess we can all figure what people are going to say. The point is, Law-Twister is still making his appeal. Go ahead, Law-Twister."

"Well . . . I asked about the Clan holding their meeting to elect a Grandfather right away," put in Mal. A small breeze came wandering by, and he felt it surprisingly cool on his forehead. Evidently there was a little perspiration up there. "One Punch here said it could be done all right, but it was a question who'd want to *suggest* it to the Clan. Naturally, he and the other grandpas who are in the running for Grandfather wouldn't like to do it. Iron Bender would have his own reasons for refusing; and Gentle Maiden here wouldn't particularly want to hold a meeting right away—"

"And we certainly shouldn't!" said Gentle Maiden. "Why go to all that trouble when here we've got Iron Bender perfectly willing and ready to tear—"

"Why, indeed?" interrupted Mal in his turn. He was beginning to get a little weary of hearing of Iron Bender's readiness to remove heads. "Except that perhaps the whole Clan deserves to be in on this—not just Iron Bender and Maiden and myself. What the Clan really ought to do is sit down and decide whether it's a good idea for the Clan to have someone like Gentle Maiden keeping three Shorties around. Does the Clan really want those Shorties to stay here? And if not, what's the best way of getting rid of these Shorties? Not that I'm trying to suggest anything to the Clan, but if the Clan should just decide to elect a Grandfather now, and the Grandfather should decide that Shorties don't qualify as orphans—"

A roar of protest from Gentle Maiden drowned him out; and a thunder of Dilbian voices arose among the seated Clan members as conversation—argument, rather, Mal told himself—became general. He waited for it to die down; but it did not. After a while, he walked over to One Punch, who was standing beside the Hill Bluffer, observing—as were two other elderly figures, obviously Grandpas Tricky and Forty Winks—but not taking part in the confusion of voices.

"One Punch," said Mal, and the oldster looked down at him cheerfully, "don't you think maybe you should quiet them down so they could hear the rest of my appeal?"

"Why, Law-Twister," said One Punch, "there's no point you going on appealing any longer, when everybody's already decided to grant what you want. They're already discussing it. Hear them?"

Since no one within a mile could have helped hearing them, there was little Mal could do but nod his head and wait. About ten minutes later, the volume of sound began to diminish as voice after voice fell silent. Finally, there was a dead silence. Members of the Clan began to reseat themselves on the grass, and from a gathering in the very center of the crowd, Gentle Maiden emerged and snorted at Mal before turning toward the village.

"I'm going to go get Bender!" she announced. "I'll get those little Shorties up here, too, so they can see Bender take care of this one and know they might just as well settle down."

She went off at a fast walk down the slope—the equivalent of about eight miles an hour in human terms.

Mal stared at One Punch, stunned.

"You mean," he asked him, "they decided not to do anything?"

A roar of explaining voices from the Clan members drowned him out and left him too deafened to understand them. When it was quiet once more, he was aware of One Punch looking severely down at him.

"Now, you shouldn't go around thinking Clan Water Gap'd talk something over and not come to some decision, Twister," he said. "Of course, they decided how it's all to go. We're going to elect a Grandfather, today."

"Fine," said Mal, beginning to revive. Then a thought struck him. "Why did Gentle Maiden go after Iron Bender just now, then? I thought—"

"Wait until you hear," said One Punch. "Clan Water Gap's come up with a decision to warm that slippery little Shorty heart of yours. You see, everyone decided, since we were going to elect a Grandfather ahead of time, that it all ought to be done in reverse."

"In reverse?"

"Why, certainly," said One Punch. "Instead of having a trial, then having the Grandfather give a decision to let you and Iron Bender hassle it out to see whether the Shorties go with you or stay with Gentle Maiden, the Clan decided to work it exactly backward."

Mal shook his head dizzily.

"I still don't understand," he said.

"I'm surprised—a Shorty like you," said One Punch, reprovingly. "I'd think backward and upside down'd be second nature to a Law-Twister. Why, what's going to happen is you and Bender'll have it out *first*, then the best decision by a grandpa'll be picked, then the grandpa who's decision's been picked will be up for election, and the Clan will elect him Grandfather."

Mal blinked.

"Decision . . ." he began feebly.

"Now, my decision," said a voice behind him, and he turned around to see that the Clan's other two elderly members had come up, "is that Iron Bender ought to win. But if he doesn't, it'll be because of some Shorty trick."

"Playing it safe, eh, Forty Winks?" said the other grandpa who had just joined them. "Well, *my* decision is that with all his tricks, and tough as we've been hearing Shorties are, that the Law-Twister can't lose. He'll chew Iron Bender up."

The two of them turned and looked expectantly at One Punch.

"Hmm," said One Punch, closing one eye and squinting thoughtfully with the other at Mal. "My decision is that the Law-Twister's even more clever and sneaky than we think. My decision says Twister'll come up with something that'll fix things his way so that they never will tangle. In short, Twister's going to win the fight even before it starts."

One Punch had turned toward the seated crowd as he

said this, and there was another low mutter of appreciation from the seated Clan members.

"That One Punch," said Grandpa Tricky to Forty Winks, "never did lay back and play it safe. He just swings right in there twice as hard as anyone else, without winking."

"Well," said One Punch himself, turning to Mal, "there's Gentle Maiden and her orphans coming up from the village now with Iron Bender. You all set, Law-Twister?"

Mal was anything but set. It was good to hear that all three grandpas of Clan Water Gap expected him to come out on top; but he would have felt a lot better if it had been Iron Bender who had been expressing that opinion. He looked over the heads of the seated crowd to see Iron Bender coming, just as One Punch had said, with Gentle Maiden and three, small, human figures in tow.

His thoughts spun furiously. This whole business was crazy. It simply could not be that in a few minutes he would be expected to engage in a hand-to-hand battle with an individual more than one and a half times his height and five times his weight, any more than it could be that the wise men of the local Clan could be betting on him to win. One Punch's prediction, in particular, was so farfetched. . . .

Understanding suddenly exploded in him. At once, it all fitted together: the Dilbian habit of circumventing any outright lie by pretending to be after just the opposite of what an individual was really after; the odd reaction of the three captured humans who had not been concerned about the Human-Hemnoid Treaty of noninterference on Dilbia when they came *into* Clan Water Gap territory, but were willing to pass up a chance of escape by letting Mal summon armed human help to rescue them, now that they were here. Just suppose—Mal thought to himself feverishly—just suppose everything is just the opposite of what it seems . . .

There was only one missing part to this whole jigsaw puzzle, one bit to which he did not have the answer. He turned to One Punch.

"Tell me something," he said, in a low voice. "Suppose Gentle Maiden and Iron Bender *had* to marry each other. Do you think they'd be very upset?"

"Upset? Well, no," said One Punch, thoughtfully. "Come to think of it, now you mention it, Law-Twister—those two are just about made for each other. Particularly seeing there's no one else made big enough or tough enough for either one of them, if you look around. In fact, if it wasn't for how they go around saying they can't stand each other, you might think they really liked each other quite a bit. Why do you ask?"

"I was just wondering," said Mal, grimly. "Let me ask you another question. Do you think a Shorty like me could carry the stone of Mighty Grappler ten paces?"

One Punch gazed at him.

"Well, you know," he said, "when it comes right down to it, I wouldn't put anything past a Shorty like you."

"Thanks," said Mal. "I'll return the compliment. Believe me, from now on, I'll never put anything past a real person like you, or Gentle Maiden, or Iron Bender, or anyone else. And I'll tell the other Shorties that when I get back among them!"

"Why thank you, Law-Twister," said One Punch. "That's mighty kind of you—but, come to think of it, maybe you better turn around now. Because Iron Bender's here."

Mal turned—just in time to see the towering figure of the village harnessmaker striding toward him, accompanied by a rising murmur of excitement from the crowd.

"All right, let's get this over with!" boomed Iron Bender, opening and closing his massive hands hungrily. "Just take me a few minutes, and then—"

"*Stop!*" shouted Mal, holding up his hand.

Iron Bender stopped, still some twenty feet from Mal. The crowd fell silent, abruptly.

"I'm sorry!" said Mal, addressing them all. "I tried every way I could to keep it from coming to this. But I see now there's no other way to do it. Now, I'm nowhere near as sure as your three grandpas that I could handle Iron Bender, here, with one hand tied behind my back. Iron Bender might well handle *me,* with no trouble. I mean, he just might be the one real man who can tangle with a Shorty like me, and win. But, what if I'm wrong?"

Mal paused, both to see how they were reacting and to get his nerve up for his next statement. If I was trying something like this any place else, he thought, they'd cart me off to a psychiatrist. But the Dilbians in front of him were all quiet and attentive, listening. Even Iron Bender and Gentle Maiden were showing no indications of wanting to interrupt.

"As I say," went on Mal, a little hoarsely as a result of working to make his voice carry to the whole assemblage, "what if I'm wrong? What if this terrific hassling ability that all we Shorties have gets the best of me when I tangle with Iron Bender? Not that Iron Bender would want me to hold back any, I know that—"

Iron Bender snorted affirmatively and worked his massive hands in the air.

"—But," said Mal, "think what the results would be. Think of Clan Water Gap without a harnessmaker. Think of Gentle Maiden here without the one real man she can't push around. I've thought about those things, and it seems to me there's just one way out. The Clan laws have to be changed so that a Shorty like me doesn't have to tangle with a Clan Gapper over this problem."

He turned to the stone of Mighty Grappler.

"So—" he wound up, his voice cracking a little on the word in spite of himself, "I'm just going to have to carry this stone ten steps so the laws can be changed."

He stepped up to the stone. There was a dead silence all around him. He could feel the sweat popping out on his face. What if the conclusions he had come to were all wrong? But he could not afford to think that now. He had to go through with the business, now that he'd spoken.

He curled his hands around the two ends of the iron rod from underneath and squatted down with his knees on either side of the rock. This was going to be different from ordinary weight lifting, where the weight was distributed on the outer two ends of the lifting bar. Here, the weight was between his fists.

He took a deep breath and lifted. For a moment, it seemed that the dead weight of the stone refused to move. Then it gave. It came up and into him until the near face of the rock thudded against his chest; the whole stone now held well off the ground.

So far, so good, for the first step. Now, for the second . . . He willed strength into his leg muscles.

Up . . . he thought to himself . . . up. . . . He could hear his teeth gritting against each other in his head. Up . . .

Slowly, grimly, his legs straightened. His body lifted, bringing the stone with it, until he stood, swaying, the weight of it against his chest, and his arms just beginning to tremble with the strain.

Now, quickly—before arms and legs gave out—he had to take the ten steps.

He swayed forward, stuck out a leg quickly, and caught himself. For a second he hung poised, then he brought the other leg forward. The effort almost overbalanced him, but he stayed upright. Now, the right foot again . . . then the left . . . the right . . . the left . . .

In the fierceness of his effort, everything else was blotted out. He was alone with the stone he had to carry, with the straining pull of his muscles, the brightness of the sun in his eyes, and the savage tearing of the rod ends on his fingers, that threatened to rip themselves out of his grip.

Eight steps . . . nine steps . . . and . . . ten!

He tried to let the stone down easily, but it thudded out of his grasp. As he stood half-bent over, it struck upright in its new resting place in the grass, then half-rolled away from him, for a moment exposing its bottom surface completely, so that he could see clearly into the hole there. Then it rocked back upright and stood still.

Painfully, stiffly, Mal straightened his back.

"Well," he panted, to the silent, staring Dilbians of Clan Water Gap, "I guess that takes care of that. . . ."

Less than forty minutes later he was herding the three anthropologists back into their shuttle boat.

"But I don't understand," protested Harvey, hesitating in the entry port of the shuttle boat. "I want to know how you got us free without having to fight that big Dilbian—the one with the name that means Iron Bender?"

"I moved their law stone," said Mal, grimly. "That meant I could change the rules of the Clan."

"But they went on and elected One Punch as Clan Grandfather, anyway," said Harvey.

"Naturally," said Mal. "He'd given the most accurate judgment in advance—he'd foretold I'd win without laying a hand on Iron Bender. And I had. Once I moved the stone, I simply added a law to the ones Mighty Grappler had set up. I said no Clan Water Gapper was allowed to adopt orphan Shorties. So, if that was against the law, Gentle Maiden couldn't keep you. She had to let you go and then there was no reason for Iron Bender to want to tangle with me."

"But why did Iron Bender and Gentle decide to get married?"

"Why, she couldn't go back to being just a single maiden again, after naming someone her protector," Mal said. "Dilbians are very strict about things like that. Public opinion *forced* them to get married—which they wanted to do anyhow, but neither of them had wanted to be the one to ask the other to marry."

Harvey blinked.

"You mean," he said disbelievingly, "it was all part of a plot by Gentle Maiden, Iron Bender, and One Punch to use us for their own advantage? To get One Punch elected Grandfather, and the other two forced to marry?"

"Now, you're beginning to understand," said Mal, grimly. He started to turn away.

"Wait," said Harvey. "Look, there's information here that you ought to be sharing with us for the sake of science—"

"Science?" Mal gave him a hard look. "That's right, it was science, wasn't it? Just pure science, that made you and your friends decide on the spur of the moment to come down here. *Wasn't it?*"

Harvey's brows drew together.

"What's that question supposed to mean?" he said.

"Just inquiring," said Mal. "Didn't it ever occur to you that the Dilbians are just as bright as you are? And that they'd have a pretty clear idea why three Shorties would show up out of thin air and start asking questions?"

"Why should that seem suspicious to them?" Ora Page stuck her face out of the entry port over Harvey's shoulder.

"Because the Dilbians take everything with a grain of salt anyway—on principle," said Mal. "Because they're experts at figuring out what someone else is really up to, since that's just the way they operate, themselves. When a Dilbian wants to go after something, his first move is to pretend to head in the opposite direction."

"They told you that in your hypnotraining?" Ora asked.

Mal shook his head.

"No," he said. "I wasn't told anything." He looked harshly at the two of them and at the face of Rice, which now appeared behind Harvey's other shoulder. "Nobody told me a thing about the Dilbians except that there are a few rare humans who understand them instinctively and can work with them, only the book-psychiatrists and the book-anthropologists can't figure out why. Nobody suggested to me that our human authorities might deliberately be trying to arrange a situation where three book-anthropologists would be on hand to observe me—as one of these rare humans—learning how to think and work like a Dilbian, on my own. No, nobody told me anything like that. It's just a Dilbian sort of suspicion I've worked out on my own."

"Look here—" began Harvey.

"You look here!" said Mal, furiously. "I don't know of anything in the Outspace Regulations that lets someone be drafted into being some sort of experimental animal without his knowing what's going on—"

"Easy now. Easy . . ." said Harvey. "All right. This whole thing was set up so we could observe you. But we had absolute faith that someone with your personality profile would do fine with the Dilbians. And, of course, you realize you'll be compensated for all this. For one thing, I think you'll find there's a full six-year scholarship waiting for you now, once you qualify for college entrance. And a few other things, too. You'll be hearing more about them when you get back to the human ambassador at Humrog Town, who sent you here."

"Thanks," said Mal, still boiling inside. "But next time tell them to ask first whether I want to play games with the rest of you! Now, you better get moving if you want to catch that spaceliner!"

He turned away. But before he had covered half a dozen steps, he heard Harvey's voice calling after him.

"Wait! There's something vitally important you didn't tell us. How did you manage to pick up that rock and carry it the way you did?"

Mal looked sourly back over his shoulder.

"I do a lot of weight lifting," he said, and kept on going.

He did not look back again; and, a few minutes later, he heard the shuttle boat take off. He headed at an angle up the valley slope behind the houses in the village toward the stone of Mighty Grappler, where the Bluffer would be waiting to take him back to Humrog Town. The sun was close to setting, and with its level rays in his eyes, he could barely make out that there were four big Dilbian figures rather than one, waiting for him by the stone. A wariness awoke in him.

When he came up, however, he discovered that the four figures were the Bluffer with One Punch, Gentle Maiden, and Iron Bender—and all four looked genial.

"There you are," said the Bluffer, as Mal stopped before him. "Better climb up into the saddle. It's not more than two hours to full dark, and even the way I travel we're going to have to move some to make it back to Humrog Town in that time."

Mal obeyed. From the altitude of the saddle, he looked over the Bluffer's right shoulder down at One Punch and Gentle Maiden and level into the face of Iron Bender.

"Well, good-bye," he said, not sure of how Dilbians reacted on parting. "It's been something, knowing you all."

"Been something for Clan Water Gap, too," replied One Punch. "I can say that now, officially, as the Clan Grandfather. Guess most of us will be telling the tale for years to come, how we got dropped in on here by the Mighty Law-Twister."

Mal goggled. He had thought he was past the point of surprise where Dilbians were concerned, but this was more than even he had imagined.

"*Mighty* Law-Twister?" he echoed.

"Why, of course," rumbled the Hill Bluffer, underneath him. "Somebody's name had to be changed, after you moved that stone."

"The postman's right," said One Punch. "Naturally, we

wouldn't want to change the name of Mighty Grappler, seeing what all he means to the Clan. Besides, since he's dead, we can't very well go around changing his name and getting folks mixed up, so we just changed yours instead. Stands to reason if you could carry Mighty Grappler's stone ten paces, you had to be pretty mighty, yourself."

"But—well, now, wait a minute . . ." Mal protested. He was remembering what he had seen in the moment he had put the stone down and it had rocked enough to let him see clearly into the hole inside it, and his conscience was bothering him. "Uh—One Punch, I wonder if I could speak to you . . . privately . . . for just a second? If we could just step over here—"

"No need for that, Mighty," boomed Iron Bender. "I and the wife are just headed back down to the village, anyway. Aren't we, Gentle?"

"Well, *I'm* going. If you want to come too—"

"That's what I say," interrupted Iron Bender. "We're both just leaving. So long, Mighty. Sorry we never got a chance to tangle. If you ever get some spare time and a good reason, come back and I'll be glad to oblige you."

"Thanks . . ." said Mal. With mixed feelings, he watched the harnessmaker and his new wife turn and stride off down the slope toward the buildings below. Then he remembered his conscience and looked again down at One Punch.

"Guess you better climb down again," the Bluffer was saying, "and I'll mosey off a few steps myself so's not to intrude."

"Now, Postman," said One Punch. "No need for that. We're all friends here. I can guess that Mighty, here, could have a few little questions to ask or things to tell—but likely it's nothing you oughtn't to hear; and besides, being a government man, we can count on you keeping any secrets."

"That's true," said the Bluffer. "Come to think of it, Mighty, it'd be kind of an insult to the government if you didn't trust me—"

"Oh, I trust you," said Mal, hastily. "It's just that . . . well . . ." He looked at One Punch. "What would you say if I told you that the stone there is hollow—that it'd been hollowed out inside?"

"Now, Mighty," said One Punch, "you mustn't make fun of an old man, now that he's become a respectable Grandfather. Anybody knows stones aren't hollow."

"But what would you say if I told you that that one is?" persisted Mal.

"Why, I don't suppose it'd make much difference you just *telling* me it was hollow," said One Punch. "I don't suppose I'd say anything. I wouldn't want folks to think you could twist me that easily, for one thing; and for another thing, maybe it might come in handy some time later, my having heard someone say that stone was hollow. Just like the Mighty Grappler said in some of his own words of wisdom— 'It's always good to have things set up one way. But it's extra good to have them set up another way, too. Two ways are always better than one.' "

"And very good wisdom that is," put in the Bluffer, admiringly. "Up near Humrog Peak there's a small bridge people been walking around for years. There *is* a kind of rumor floating around that it's washed out in the middle, but I've never heard anybody really say so. Never know when it might come in useful to have a bridge like that around for someone who'd never heard the rumor—that is, if there's any truth to the rumor, which I doubt."

"I see," said Mal.

"Of course you do, Mighty," said One Punch. "You understand things real well for a Shorty. Now, luckily we don't have to worry about this joke of yours that the stone of Mighty Grappler is hollow, because we've got proof otherwise."

"Proof?" Mal blinked.

"Why, certainly," said One Punch. "Now, it stands to reason, if that stone were hollow, it wouldn't be anywhere near as heavy as it looks. In fact, it'd be real light."

"That's right," said Mal, sharply. "And you saw me—a Shorty—pick it up and carry it."

"Exactly!" said One Punch. "The whole Clan was watching to see you pick that stone up and carry it. And we did."

"And that proves it isn't hollow?" Mal stared.

"Why sure," said One Punch. "We all saw you sweating and struggling and straining to move that stone just ten paces. Well, what more proof does a man need? If it'd been hollow like you say, a Shorty—let alone a mighty Shorty like you—would've been able to pick it up with one paw and just stroll off with it. But we were watching you closely, Mighty, and you didn't leave a shred of doubt in the mind of any one of us that it was just about all you could carry. So, that stone just *had* to be solid."

He stopped. The Bluffer snorted.

"You see there, Mighty?" the Bluffer said. "You may be a real good law-twister—nobody doubts it for a minute—but when you go up against the wisdom of a real elected Grandfather, you find you can't twist him like you can any ordinary real man."

"I . . . guess so," said Mal. "I suppose there's no point, then, in my suggesting you just take a look at the stone?"

"It'd be kind of beneath me to do that, Mighty," said

One Punch, severely, "now that I'm a Grandfather and already pointed out how it couldn't be hollow, anyway. Well, so long."

Abruptly, as abruptly as Iron Bender and Gentle Maiden had gone, One Punch turned and strode off down the slope.

The Hill Bluffer turned on one heel, himself, and strode away in the opposite direction, into the mountains and the sunset.

"But the thing I don't understand," said Mal to the Bluffer, a few minutes later when they were back on the narrow trail, out of sight of Water Gap Territory, "is how . . . What would have happened if those three Shorties hadn't dropped in the way they did? And what if I hadn't been sent for? One Punch might have been elected Grandfather anyway, but how would Iron Bender and Gentle Maiden ever have gotten married?"

"Lot of luck to it all, I suppose you could say, Mighty," answered the Bluffer, sagely. "Just shows how things turn out. Pure chance—like my mentioning to Little Bite a couple of months ago it was a shame there hadn't been other Shorties around to watch just how the Half-Pint Posted and Pick-and-Shovel did things, back when they were here."

"You . . ." Mal stared, "mentioned . . ."

"Just offhand, one day," said the Bluffer. "Of course, as I told Little Bite, there weren't hardly any real champions around right now to interest a tough little Shorty—except over at Clan Water Gap, where my unmarried cousin Gentle Maiden lived."

"Your *cousin*. . . ? I see," said Mal. There was a long, long pause. "Very interesting."

"Funny. That's how Little Bite put it, when I told him,"

answered the Bluffer, cat-footing confidently along the very edge of a precipice. "You Shorties sure have a habit of talking alike and saying the same things all the time. Comes of having such little heads with not much space inside for words, I suppose."

Three Blind Mice

INTRODUCTION

A crash landing on a frozen planet. Inscrutable alien creatures bent on killing the men of the Terran Space Command. Keith Laumer has put together all the juicy morsels of an action-adventure feast.

But look again. The three humans are a curious blend of strengths and weaknesses. And the aliens have some strange problems of their own.

Formerly an Air Force captain and a State Department Foreign Officer, Keith Laumer has become one of the most productive and popular writers of science fiction. Tall, dashing, and as vigorous as any adventure-story hero, he lives in a beautifully modernistic home in Florida that he built himself, next to a lake that is home for at least one alligator.

His novels include Time Trap, Long Twilight, *and* House in November. *His short stories are legion. Most famous of all, perhaps, are his many stories about Reteif, an interstellar diplomat who is not adverse to making action speak louder than rhetoric.*

But behind all the action and adventure, there is a keen sense of where it's at, as witnessed here in "Three Blind Mice."

by KEITH LAUMER

As Cameron recovered consciousness, the first thing he was aware of was pain: the sting of cuts and bruises, the searing sensation of a burn that had scorched his left forearm, a dull ache spreading from his lower back. The second datum he absorbed was that the three-man scout boat was in free fall toward the glaring surface of the planet, looming on the screen before his padded command chair.

His mind raced back over the final moments before unconsciousness. He remembered the sighting of the Yrax cruiser as it had emerged from the radar shadow of the uninhabited ice-giant planet, behind which he had stationed his tiny spy ship. The great war vessel had apparently detected the presence of the intruding Terrans at the same moment. Its instant response had been a salvo capable of blasting a battleship into its component atoms.

Which it might well have done, had the target been a battleship, massive and sluggish. But even as the Yrax missiles leaped forth, Cameron had stood the tiny ship on its stern and blasted it from the line of fire at full 9-G acceleration. The scout ship had pitched and bucked in the shockwaves as massive detonations ripped the space it had occupied seconds before; but it had righted itself with a scream of overstressed gyros and streaked outward. Though its crew lay stunned by the violence of the maneuvers, its recorders whined efficiently as they abstracted precious data on Yrax firepower and cruise capability from the frantically maneuvering warship—data which had until now been an absorbing mystery to Terran Space Command.

The war—if so one-sided a conflict could be called a war—was in its third year; four Terran colonies had been attacked and wiped out to the last man. Two dozen Terran freighters had been blasted from space with no survivors. Six revenue cutters of the Terran Space Arm had been jumped and vaporized without warning. Seven mining installations had been reduced to radioactive dust. And still, absolutely nothing was known of the enemy who struck so swiftly and so ruthlessly—nothing but their name, the Yrax, gleaned from intercepted transmissions in an unknown tongue, badly garbled by star static, attenuated by the vast distances of interstellar space.

And now, Cameron realized, he and his two-man crew had encountered a Yrax warship—and were still alive to report their findings—so far.

The planet below was less than five hundred miles distant, if the mass/proximity indicator was reading accurately. The ship's velocity was over 20,000 kilometers per hour, relative, fortunately at a tangent to the planetary surface. Already the first whistlings of attenuated outer atmosphere were setting up resonant vibrations in the vessel's eternalloy hull. Cameron keyed the autopilot into action. At once the braking jets flared, filling the screens with their pale fire.

Beside him, Lucas, the engineer, leaned groggily over the auxiliary panel, his face barely visible in the dim glow of the instruments.

"Luke—you okay?" Cameron called over the sibilant shrill

of the thin gasses that buffeted and tore at the hurtling boat. The engineer pulled himself upright and glanced his way; his teeth showed in a brief, encouraging grin. On Cameron's right, Navigator Wybold stirred, groaned, opened his eyes, sat up.

"We're going to hit," Cameron said. "But maybe we've got enough stuff left to cushion the crunch. How're you feeling, Wy?"

"Okay—I hope," the navigator said. "How about you, Jim?"

"Still breathing," Cameron said. He studied the instrument array, forming a mental picture of the vast planet spreading below: the great ice fields, the serrated ridges of mountain ranges thrusting up like bared teeth into the dense, turbulent atmosphere. At less than one hundred miles from the surface, the broken scout boat hurtled in a long descending arc, slicing deeper into the gases of the upper stratosphere.

"We're starting to warm up," Lucas said in a clipped emotionless tone. "Hull temperature 900° and climbing fast. But so far our refrigeration gear is holding it."

"Try to put a little axial spin on us, Luke," Cameron said.

"I've only got about 25 percent control of the steering jets," Lucas said, "but I'll see what I can do."

There was a surge, as the boat responded to the spurt of energy from the small-attitude jets mounted equatorily around its hull. The panel seemed to sink away, slide sideways, rise, fall back in a nauseous gyration.

"Not so good," Lucas said. "We're spinning, but with a bad wobble. I'd better let it go at that. Another shot might put us into a full-fledged tumble."

"Luke—switch on the stern screen, will you?" Cameron

ordered. The engineer fine-focused the foot-square aft viewer. Against the blackness of space, partly obscured by whipping swirls and streamers of exhaust gases, a brilliant point of light glared. Cameron saw the muscles at the corner of the engineer's square-cut jaw knot hard.

"They're following us down," he said. "Those critters don't intend to take any chances at all, do they?"

"They can't afford to—not with what we've got on our record spools," Wybold said.

"Well, maybe we'll fool them," Cameron stated flatly. "There's a lot of real estate down there to get lost in. Let's see what we can do."

Ahead, a range of knife-edged mountains towered ten miles into the eroding millrace that was the ice giant's atmosphere. Cameron jockeyed the thrust controls with a delicate touch, holding the boat prow-first in the direction of travel, using the malfunctioning steering jets to aim for the deep-cut V, like a wedge chopped by a mighty ax in the wall of jagged stone and ice. Now the peaks to left and right were above them, ripping past, aglitter in the white glare of the distant sun. A great slope of black stone rushed toward them, directly in their path. Lucas slammed full power to the remaining starboard tubes; there was a brief flare of energy, a bone-wrenching surge—then the damaged steering engines flashed in an instant to white heat. A spray of metal vapor engulfed the boat as the automatic safety circuits blasted the explosive bolts securing them to the vessel. Light flared on the screens as the jettisoned engines detonated half a mile astern. Then a crashing, clanging impact, a long, tearing screech of tortured metal that went on and on—

And then, amazingly, silence, and the absence of all motion.

A fitful wind whined over the broken hull. Escaping air hissed thinly. Hot metal *pinged!* contracting. The heaters hummed, attempting to maintain a livable temperature.

Moving slowly, painfully, Cameron looked around the compartment. His couch was half-ripped from its moorings. A tangle of wiring and fluid conduits had bulged from the shattered control console. Beside him, the bulkhead was creased out of shape.

"Where are we, Wy?" he asked the navigator.

"We're down on a continental ice mass about fifty kilometers north of the estimated equator, a couple of hundred kilometers from a big sea to the north. We're about two thousand meters above nominal sea level; my range readings as we came in were kind of confused.

"We're in a high valley; peaks on all sides. Outside temperature, 210 absolute. Gravity, 1.31 standard. Air pressure, 23 psi; composition, nitrogen 85%, oxygen 10%, some water vapor. Wind velocity, 20 m.p.h. gusting to 50. It seems to be high noon; this sun radiates strongly in the upper end of the visible spectrum and in the UV, and it's pretty bright out there. It reminds me a little of Vera Cruz in that respect." He smiled briefly at the comparison of his beloved desert world with this frozen wasteland.

"I never did understand why anybody wanted to colonize that sandbox," Lucas mused, eyeing Wybold obliquely. "I suppose some people will try anything, though."

"Right—like settling down on a high-G world like Sandow, where you have to be a champion weight lifter just to walk around," Wybold replied with a ghost of a smile.

"And it looks like we'll be walking," Lucas said bluntly. "Hull broached, main power out, auxiliary power out, emergency power at 10 percent base capability. Communications out—super-E, infrawave, SWF—the works." He shook his head. "However, I got off an all-wave Mayday, before we broke through the troposphere," he added casually.

Cameron managed a grin. "I'm glad you weren't too busy adjusting the air conditioning to see to that detail."

"Hard to say what good it will do us," Lucas said. "We're a long way from the nearest Terran base." He turned to the dark cockpit display screens, flipped switches. There was no response.

"Try the DV's," Cameron suggested. Wybold fitted his face to the padded eyepiece and turned the dials which focused the direct vision scopes. He squinted into the dazzling light reflecting from the icefield—bright enough to be painful even to his insensitive vision, adapted to the blazing sunlight of his homeworld. Steep escarpments rose to either side of the long valley; against the glaring pale blue sky, a single point of brilliance winked and flickered.

"Oh-oh," he said. "They're still with us. We'll have dropped off their radar and gamma-tracer screens—but we'll show up like a bonfire on IR. If they haven't pinpointed us yet, they will any minute."

"We'll have to get out," Cameron said. "They'll blow the boat off the map. We can hole up in the rocks, maybe."

Lucas unstrapped, rose to his feet, his muscular bulk making his thick body look short in spite of his six-foot-one height. He turned to the suit locker, lifted out Cameron's suit, tossed Wybold's to him, pulled out his own.

Cameron had swiveled the DV eyepiece around, reduced the light level, and was studying the scene.

"Broken ground up ahead," he said. "Caves. That's the spot to make for."

"Sure. Better get that suit on, Jim. It's cold out there."

Cameron shook his head. "Sorry, Luke. You and Wy get moving. I'll sit tight and give them a little surprise as they close in—"

"What are you trying to do, get a medal out of this, Jim?" Lucas said. "Come on—time's a-wasting."

Cameron shook his head.

"What's this—the old captain-goes-down-with-his-ship routine?"

"My back's sprained," Cameron said. "I can't move my legs."

"Wy, let's help Jim get into his suit," Lucas said briskly.

"You're wasting time," Cameron said as the two set to work, moving clumsily in their suits, hampered by the massive tug of the big planet.

"They won't try to land that big baby," Lucas said. "She'd break up in this G-field. That means they'll have to send a shore party down in a sideboat. That will take awhile. Wy, let's unclamp my couch for a stretcher."

"That's just more extra weight," Cameron protested.

"Pile it on," Lucas said. "That's what these piano legs are for." Working swiftly, the two men freed the couch and placed the injured man in it, strapping him in securely.

Outside, Cameron looked back at the battered hull, half sunk in the frozen snow at the end of the long trough it had scored in landing.

"Take a last look," he said. "She was a good boat, but

she'll never lift again—and neither will we, if we don't get out of sight in a hurry." He glanced at Lucas and saw that the big man's eyes were tight shut. Tears trickled down his cheek and froze.

"Hey, Luke—don't take it so hard," he started, only half jokingly.

"Sorry," Lucas said, opening his eyes just far enough for the navigator to see that they were enflamed and red. "I'm afraid I can't take the light. I'm snow-blind."

Wybold hesitated only for a moment. Then he stepped forward, freed a harness strap, and clipped it to a D-ring on the engineer's belt, linking them.

"Follow the leader," he said, and started up the long slope—to his desert-conditioned eyes just pleasantly illuminated—toward the jumbled rocks and the dark cave mouths a quarter of a mile away.

They had covered three quarters of the distance, when Cameron suddenly called, "Duck!"

In total silence, the Yrax gunboat rocketed into view from behind them, streaked low overhead, trailed by a deafening sonic boom that shook snow loose from the high ridges all around. In an instant, the air was filled with the rumble of sliding ice. The ground trembled underfoot, as immense glacial fragments dislodged by the sudden shock detached themselves from the slopes and started downward, driving whirling clouds of loose snow ahead.

"Run for it," Wybold shouted over the thunder, and putting his head down, he ran, with Lucas close behind.

In a blinding fog of whirling ice crystals, the men scaled the jumble of rock, searching for a cranny big enough to conceal them. They reached the top of the first incline, found a narrow ledge leading to the left and upward between high walls—a route cut by ages of runoff water from spring thaws.

"It might be a dead end," Wybold said. "What do you think, Jim?"

"We'll try it, Wy. We don't have much choice."

Even the navigator's desert-trained vision, developed on a world where blazing sunlight and obscuring dust storms were a way of life, were of little value now. He climbed doggedly on, feeling his way up the narrow trail. There was a sharp turn, and the ravine widened into a bowl-shaped hollow—possibly an old lake basin—the walls of which were riddled with shallow, water-cut grottoes. Most of these were far too small to shelter a man, and all were choked with ice. But ahead, on the right, a single black opening showed. Wybold struggled across the drifts toward it. It was a cave, its mouth protected by a narrow passage. It seemed clear, but to Wybold the interior was only an inky blackness.

"Luke—can you make out anything in there?"

The engineer moved up beside him, blinked his light-burned eyes, grateful for the soothing gloom.

"A small opening, but it widens out inside. Goes back a good twenty feet and turns. It'll do."

Inside, Lucas deposited Cameron's improvised cot in a sheltered spot well back from the entrance.

"All the comforts of home, gentlemen," he said.

"Better check out the back of the cave," Cameron said to Lucas. "There may be another way in."

Lucas nodded and set off, moving surely in the near-darkness.

"What do you suppose their plan of attack will be, Jim?"

Wybold asked, scanning the expanse of dazzling white visible beyond the opening.

"If they're smart, they'll bring up some kind of heavy gun and blast away," Cameron replied. "But if they're smarter, they'll try to come in on foot and make sure of us."

"We'll know pretty soon," Wybold said.

The rearmost extension of the cave, Lucas found, though it narrowed sharply, did not pinch off entirely. Concealed in deep shadow, an opening some six feet high and barely two feet in width split the rock wall. To ordinary vision, the darkness beyond would have been impenetrable; but to the Sandovian's sensitive eyes a twisting tunnel was dimly visible, leading back into the cliff. In ages past, Lucas guessed, during a warmer age in the life of the big planet, thawing ice had eroded this route down through the stone, which in turn implied an unguarded access at the far end. For a moment, he considered returning to report on his finding and request permission to continue; then, he squeezed his powerful bulk through the narrow aperture and, ducking slightly under low clearance, prowled along the passage into the rock.

Almost at once, the way angled sharply upward, became an almost vertical shaft through tumbled rock. Climbing was difficult; the water-worn stones were smoothly rounded, hard to grip. After a dozen feet, the narrowing tunnel leveled off, became a wide, low-ceilinged shelf. Lucas was forced to lie flat and crawl, using fingers and toes.

The ceiling shelved gradually downward, closing in. When it was apparent that no more progress could be made dead ahead, he angled to the right. At once, he found himself wedged tight between floor and ceiling. With an arm-creaking effort, he pulled himself through and the passage opened out. Through a gap in the rock ahead, watery daylight leaked.

Lucas crawled forward, shielding his eyes from the light, saw a final, irregularly-walled crevice leading out to the open. He made his way along it, emerged on a windswept slope of frozen snow, bathed in the deep blue shadow of an ice peak. Here, out of the direct sunlight, he was able to see, though painfully. He made a narrow aperture between his fingers, striving to make out the details of the scene below. He was, he determined, at a point some fifty yards above and to the left of the cave mouth—a spot inaccessible to any climber from below. At his back, a vertical ice wall rose. As he was about to turn away, there was a sound from below. Motion caught his eye, below and to the left. He went flat, watched as a sticklike creature, moving quickly on four multiple-jointed legs, rounded a shoulder of ice and poised on the narrow ledge leading along the cliff face, its flexible torso curving upward in an attitude of alert listening. Four additional limbs sprang from the alien's shoulder region, the lower pair long, tipped with paired chelae, the upper pair short, flexible as a monkey's tail. The body was the color of blued steel, with a hard, polished look. Straps crisscrossed the narrow thorax, bearing badges and pouches.

For the first time, a human being was looking at a Yrax soldier.

The alien stood for a moment, the stiff, antennalike members atop its insignificant, bullet-shaped head moving restlessly. Then, it darted forward. From his vantage point above, Lucas saw the narrow cleft in the ice lying directly in the Yrax's path. The Yrax, however, scanning the slopes above, failed to notice the trap. As its forelegs went over the edge, the long arms shot out, scored the ice on the far side in a vain bid for purchase. But the weight of the massive body was too great. Ice chips flew as the rear legs clawed, resisting the inexorable slide. Then the heavy torso slid down, dropped into the crevasse. For another few seconds the creature clung, while its arms raked desperately for a grip. Then, with a final screech of iron-hard claws on ice, it was gone, clattering away into the depths to lodge with a smash far below.

At the same moment, a second Yrax appeared around the abutment. It moved briskly forward, paused for a moment at the edge of the cleft, then raised its upper body and lunged across the yard-wide gap. For a moment it seemed as though it might be safe, then the forward pair of legs—which had gained a precarious purchase on the rim of ice—slipped back. As the creature clung by its forelimbs—it had secured a better grip than its predecessor—two more Yrax came into view along the path. One veered to the right, the other to the left. Neither took any apparent notice of their fellow, still clinging to his precarious hold on safety.

One of the newcomers edged to his left along the cleft to the edge of the narrow ledge it cut. It leaned out to examine the terrain below, but seemingly found nothing there to encourage it. Moving back a few feet, it sprang forward, cleared the cleft in a bound, landing with a metallic clatter, but safely, only its hind pair of legs kicking fragments of ice free from the lip of the pitfall as it pulled itself forward and disappeared from Lucas' view.

Meanwhile, the second newcomer had explored to its right, moving out of Lucas' line of sight. He heard the scrape of the horny limbs on ice, a clatter, the sounds of falling ice chunks, then a distant crashing. The creature did not reappear.

As a fourth Yrax advanced along the ledge, the unfortunate advance guard who had been silently dangling above the abyss slipped suddenly, dropped from view. Lucas winced at the now-familiar sound of impact far below. And now more of the aliens were appearing, some scouting along the edge, some launching themselves without hesitation, some crossing the gap, others falling to unnoticed death. A few turned aside, began exploring the wall to their right. If they found a route there, Lucas realized, the rear entrance to the cave would be quickly discovered.

He eased back silently from the edge, studied the opening in the rock. It was not large, but would be obvious at even a casual glance. It would have to be camouflaged. That meant snow and ice—the only materials available.

Lucas' eyes were burning, closing in spite of his efforts to keep them open. He clambered up above the opening, then set his feet against a large block of packed snow, and pushed.

The results exceeded his expectations. The crust broke away suddenly; a slab of ice ten feet long and a yard high toppled over the edge to thud massively down before the narrow entrance—and Lucas, deprived abruptly of his grip, slid after it. He struck hard, a jagged edge of ice smashing across his ribs with stunning force. He was dimly aware of the impact of ice fragments around him, of the whirl of loose snow driven up by the displaced air, of a distant, ominous rumble.

Then something struck his head, and all thought faded into swirling darkness.

In the cave, Wybold cocked his head, listening to the muffled rumbling that seemed to come from deep inside the mountain. A sudden gust of air puffed from the dark recesses at the rear of the deep cave, bringing with it a scattering of snow crystals. The sound died away; the fitful draft dwindled and was gone. Only a long drift of powdery snow across the floor attested to the brief flurry. Wybold turned; his eyes met Cameron's.

"Sounded like a cave-in," the injured man said.

"I'd better go have a look," the navigator said. Neither man mentioned the thought uppermost on their minds: *Lucas is back there somewhere. . . .*

"You'll be as blind in the dark as Luke is in direct sunlight," Cameron said bluntly.

"I can feel my way. Don't forget my famous Veracrucian sense of direction." He tried to make the words sound light.

"Move me over beside the front door before you go," Cameron said.

Wybold paused. "I wasn't thinking," he said. "Of course I can't leave you here alone."

"I have my suit gun," Cameron said. "Just prop me up so I can see down that passage."

"Wait a minute, Jim—"

"Luke might be needing help pretty badly, Wy," Cameron cut him off. "Better hurry up."

Five minutes later, with the crippled Cameron settled in position guarding the entrance, Wybold set off along the path Lucas had followed. At first, the route was clear enough; he slipped easily through the cleft in the rock, moving forward by feeling his way with outstretched hands, sliding his feet forward to explore for unseen pitfalls. At the point where the route angled upward, he was baffled for awhile; then he found the opening leading upward and began to climb.

In the low chamber where Lucas had almost become wedged, Wybold paused for breath. In total darkness and utter stillness, he lay on his face under the shelving rock, before starting on. Directly before him, the ceiling dipped sharply. Lucas could never have negotiated that passage, the navigator felt sure. But had he gone right, or left?

Either direction seemed equally likely. Wybold chose the left. The space widened until he could rise to all fours, then to his feet, though it was still necessary to stoop. Through his open faceplate, he felt a steady flow of cold, fresh air. Feeling his way toward its source, he saw a faint glow of daylight that widened out into a steeply angled cut leading up to a strip of vivid blue sky.

It was a difficult climb up the twenty-foot slope of icy rock; but at last he reached the top and emerged on a slope of glittering snow beneath a towering crag. A ragged edge of broken snow crust ran just below his position, as from a recent snowslide. The stretch of bare rock thus exposed ended in an abrupt dropoff. Beyond and below this edge, strange figures moved.

Wybold dropped flat, watching the Yraci scouts as they scurried back and forth, exploring the extent of a great drift of broken ice blocking the ledge along which they made their separate ways. One clambered directly up the side of the heap, slipped as he neared the top, rolled helplessly back down, and disappeared over the edge. Others climbed up at other points; some succeeded in negotiating the obstruction, and hurried away long the ledge; others tumbled back to the base, back near their starting point and immediately tried again. Still others followed the one who had fallen over the side. None appeared to be aware of the efforts of his fellows. There was no particular effort to follow in the tracks of the successful climbers or to shun the routes that led to catastrophe.

For ten minutes, Wybold watched the procession. A few stragglers arrived, picked their routes, fell or passed the blockage. One last multilegged alien hurried up, skittered upslope, clattered down safely on the far side and was gone. The navigator waited another two minutes, then cautiously rose and worked his way downslope. It was an eight-foot drop to the top of the ice heap blocking the ledge. As he debated attempting the risky descent, with the idea of following the alien scouting party, he noticed a small patch of dark blue visible through the heaped ice dust—a blue of the identical shade of a regulation Space Arm ship suit.

"Luke!" he exclaimed. In a moment Wybold had turned, lowered himself over the edge, and dropped. He struck the ice heap near its crest, caught himself as he slipped toward the adjacent chasm, and slid down beside the place where the telltale color gleamed through the drift. Quickly, he raked away the loose ice chips, lifted a larger slab aside, and exposed the engineer's left arm.

The buried man was in no immediate danger of suffocation—provided the faceplate of his suit had been closed. And the layer of fallen ice and snow did not seem to be deep enough to have done any serious damage. But Lucas lay ominously still.

Wybold cleared his arm to the shoulder, exposed his head, and breathed a sigh of relief as he saw that Lucas' faceplate was closed. Five more minutes' work had cleared the unconscious man's torso. At that point, Lucas stirred. Wybold looked back down along the ledge; the route the

Yraci had used was marked by their many-limbed tracks that wound back down toward the snowfield below. Ahead, the route curved out of sight. No aliens were in view, but they could return at any moment.

"Luke! Wake up," Wybold urged. "We've got to get out of sight!"

Two minutes later Lucas was on his feet, groggy from the blow a thirty-pound ice fragment had dealt him, but able to walk.

"They've gone on along the ledge, toward the cave mouth," Wybold told him. "Let's get going. Jim's holding the fort alone."

Lucas looked up at the ice-rimmed ledge above. "I'll boost you up," he said. He squatted and Wybold stepped up; after a brief scramble, he pulled himself to the top.

"Hard work in this G," Wy panted. Lying flat, he extended an arm to the engineer. Lucas found a small foothold, reached up as far as he was able. His hand was a foot short of Wybold's outstretched hand. He found a precarious handhold, pulled himself up a few inches, but slipped back.

"No go," he said. "You go on back, Wy. I'll trail our friends and keep an eye on them. Maybe I can create a diversion—"

"Uh-uh," Wybold shook his head. "I can't see my hand in front of my face in there. I almost got lost in that maze. I'd never find my way back. And as for you keeping a watch —you can't see any better out here than I can inside. We'll stick together and watch for a break." He slipped over the edge and dropped back down beside Lucas.

"All right," the engineer said. "Let's go see what they're up to."

Alone in the icy cave, settled as comfortably as his wrenched back would allow, Cameron had lain for the better part of an hour, sighting along the barrel of the weapon propped on the stone before him. The afternoon sun glared frosty white on the patch of snow visible beyond the opening twenty feet away. Even his Earth-normal vision was beginning to suffer from the continual strain; he blinked and turned away to rest his eyes. When he looked back, an ungainly silhouette stood poised against the light.

For a long moment, neither Cameron nor the intruder moved. The Yrax seemed to be studying the dark recess, considering its next move. Suddenly it stepped forward on its four slim legs, lowering its upraised torso to duck under the entry. Cameron waited. The Yrax advanced cautiously. When it was ten feet away, it saw him. For a moment, it halted; then, it gathered its legs and crouched. Cameron took careful aim at the point of juncture of the slim neck and the horny thorax and pressed the switch of the heat gun. A brilliant point of light glinted on the alien's shiny blue-black exoderm. In the blue-white glare, smoke puffed outward from the point of contact. The creature leaped backward, its carapace raking the sides of the entry with a metallic clatter, and was gone. A rank odor of charred horn hung in the air.

Cameron uttered a harsh sigh and blinked at sweat that had trickled into his eyes. He resighted the gun and waited, looking out at stillness and silence. And, suddenly, another Yrax was framed in the entry.

This time Cameron didn't wait. The beam lanced out, seared a smoking blister on the chitinous thorax. As before, the victim recoiled, skittered from sight, apparently unharmed.

Two Yraci arrived simultaneously. One thrust ahead; the heat beam caught him, and he leaped back but collided with his fellow. For a frantic moment, the two aliens threshed, limbs entangled, while Cameron raked them indiscriminately. Then both tumbled away, darted from view.

After that, there was a lull that stretched on for half a minute, a full minute. . . .

Abruptly, an alien was there, staggering under the burden of a massive shape of dull metal, which it deposited squarely in the entrance. It set swiftly to work, adjusting the apparatus, so that a series of what appeared to be ring sights were squarely aligned along the dim tunnel. At this range—the Yrax was some twenty-five feet distant—the diverging beam of the heat projector cast a disk of light that was barely visible in the glare of the sun, and seemed to discomfit the alien not at all as it busied itself at its task. Cameron shifted aim, directing his beam at the cluster of what he guessed to be the controls of the alien machine. In seconds the iodine-colored metal glowed red hot. Moments later—as the Yrax gunner squatted, multiple knees beside the armored body, to sight along the firing tube—the weapon burst with a sharp detonation that sent its operator flying in a cloud of ice chips. As the smoke of the explosion cleared, Cameron saw that the body of the device had burst, exposing coils of wiring that burned with a fierce light that suggested pure magnesium. In the next five minutes, he fired on three more Yraci who came forward as if to inspect the ruined gun. Their reactions never varied from the pattern: immediate flight.

Then a lull. Ten minutes passed. Somewhere far away Cameron heard a low rumble, as of distant cannon fire.

Then nothing. Slowly, the shadows lengthened. Cameron waited.

From a concealed ledge a hundred yards above the cave mouth, Lucas and Wybold had watched as the aliens crawled over the tumbled moraine of rock and ice, poking into one cave mouth after another. They had seen an alien halt before the cave where they knew Cameron waited, alone and hurt, watched as the intruder started in, then tumbled out in obvious distress. They had observed as others made the attempt, ignored by their fellows, who continued to poke and probe into other dark recesses in the rock. When the weapon-bearing Yrax came up, they had tensed to jump to their feet, shout, anything to distract the gunner. But the machine had suddenly winked with blue-white light, and an instant later the sharp crack of the detonation reached their ears.

"He's holding them off," Wybold said. "But it can't go on forever."

"They don't know much about cooperation," Lucas said. "Look at that one—he's going to bring that whole ridge right down on his pals—" As he spoke, a long rim of ice which had precariously overhung the floor of the hollow broke away, came crashing down, raising the inevitable cloud of snow and ice crystals. At once, Wybold saw the opportunity. He scrambled to his feet.

"Luke—come on—while they're blinded!" He plunged forward, half slid, half fell down the slope. He came upright in a white mist as opaque as milk glass, and paused for a moment, attuning his directional sense.

"This way, Luke," he called, and plunged ahead. He dodged past the dimly-seen figure of a Yrax, groping through the murk, and skirted a mound of fallen ice; then the cave mouth opened before him. He floundered through a waist-deep drift, gained the entry.

"Jim! It's me!" he shouted. Then he was beside Cameron, who reached out to grip his hand.

"I knew you clowns had something to do with that snowstorm out there," the injured man called over the now diminishing roar. "Where's Luke?"

Wybold whirled. "He was right behind me—"

"Wait!" Cameron's voice checked him. "You can't go back out there, Wy! They'll spot you! The snow is already settling!"

"But—Luke . . ."

"Luke knows where we are," Cameron said. "He'll expect to find us here."

"I guess you're right," Wybold concurred reluctantly.

When Wybold shouted and disappeared into the obscuring whirl of snow, Lucas lowered his head against the blinding glare and charged after him. He fell almost at once, regained his feet, fell again. A massive ice block crashed down directly in his path; he veered to the left, recoiled as the ungainly shape of a Yrax appeared before him, in distress as obvious as his own. It ignored him, blundered past, and Lucas went on, climbing the drifts, falling, picking himself up. . . .

The ground was rising; Lucas paused, picturing the lay of the land as he had dimly seen it from above. There was no upward slope between his point of departure and the cave mouth. And he sensed that he had gone too far. He had covered a hundred feet at least, and the distance to the entry had been no more than seventy at most.

Vaguely now, he could see a slope of craggy ice rising above him. No more ice was falling from above. He looked back. The obscuring veil was settling. Vague shapes moved in the hollow below. In another moment he would be in plain view to the aliens. He resumed his climb, pulled himself up into a shallow gully, turned to scan the back trail. He saw the cave mouth now, half buried in snow. He had missed it by fifty feet. At least twenty Yraci prowled the ledge before it. Wybold was not in sight. That was good, Lucas told himself; he would be inside with Jim now.

And he was outside.

For half an hour, Lucas watched the apparently aimless movements of the aliens. Many of them attempted to scale the slopes that enclosed the ledge on three sides. All failed —which did not deter others from attempting the same task. Along the lower trail—the single access to the hollow, now that the upper trail was blocked—more aliens arrived, to repeat the performances of their predecessors. Then they settled down in apparent patience before the cave mouth.

"Stalemate," Lucas muttered to himself. "They can't get inside, and Jim and Wy can't get out. And if they could, the escape route's blocked. The only way out leads right into the arms of the Yraci." For another quarter of an hour he studied the scene, as the sun, obscured now behind a peak, sank swiftly lower, bringing a twilight that was soothing to the man's burning eyes.

Can't stay here, he thought. Temperature's already falling. Have to do something . . .

A trickle of snow slid down from the slope above the cave to form a low mound in the open trail. A lone Yrax, a late arrival, clambered up over it, leaving a busy trail of foot and drag marks, hurried on to join the waiting group before the cave. Bunched up as they were, they offered a perfect target for a few well-aimed rounds of artillery fire, Lucas reflected. All that was lacking was the artillery.

The engineer tensed suddenly, frowning in thought. Then he rose, moved silently along the gully until he had traversed the crest of the ridge. Below, the last gleam of dusk lit the long valley. Keeping to the high ground, Lucas set off at a brisk walk directly away from the cave.

"Getting cold out there," Wybold said. "Luke can't take a night out in the open. Maybe I'd better go look for him."

"To you, it's been pitch dark for an hour, Wy," Cameron said. "You couldn't see your hand in front of your face. Anyway, Luke will expect us to sit tight. If there's anything he can do, he'll do it."

"I feel pretty useless, just sitting here."

"I know how you feel," Cameron said. "But let's not make the mistake our pals the Yraci do."

"What do you mean?"

"They don't work together. We do. And our part of the job right now is just staying put."

"Maybe, Jim. But what if Luke can't reach the back door? What if he's waiting for us to come out that way?"

"Wy—we're both blind in a dark cave. And you aren't a Sandovian like Luke. You couldn't lug me that far on your back."

"I suppose you're right."

I hope so, Cameron thought.

The diffuse starlight lit the scene comfortably for Lucas. He made good time, coming stealthily down on the wrecked scout boat from above after a brisk twenty-minute hike. It was nearly buried in the snow that was shaken down by the sonic boom of the Yraci landing craft. There were a maze of alien footprints around it; trails led away across the snow in the direction of the cave. But no aliens were in sight.

Lucas set to work, digging the soft drifts away from the hull, at a point fifteen feet from the exposed stern. In a quarter of an hour, he had excavated a pit six feet deep and wide enough to stand in, with a minimum of elbow room. Against the curve of hull thus revealed, the rounded bulge of a steering engine housing flared. The inspection cover unsnapped easily. The engine itself was an eighteen-inch-long torpedo shape, blunt at both ends, attached to its gimbaled mountings by four heavy-duty retaining clamps. They were designed to be loosened quickly; steering engine replacement had sometimes to be made in space, under difficult conditions. In the tool locker inside the boat, there was a special wrench for the purpose; but the hatch was buried now under tons of ice. If the clamps were to be removed, it would have to be by hand.

Lucas dug away more packed snow to give his feet good purchase. He planted himself, gripped the big knurled knob in one hand, closed the other hand over it, and applied pressure. His grip slipped. He squeezed harder, threw every ounce of power in his big frame into the effort. With a sharp *crack!* the clamp spun free.

The second and third clamps turned more easily. The last was balky, but on the third try—an effort that made tiny bright lights whirl before Lucas' eyes—it yielded. Carefully, he disconnected the control leads; if they were accidentally crossed, the engine would ignite at once, ejecting a 2 cm. stream of superheated ions at a velocity of 2,000 feet per second—and incidentally pulverizing anyone in the vicinity. He lifted the massive engine down—its Earth-normal weight was 240 pounds—cradled it in his arms, and started back toward the cave.

* * *

The hike back was not so easy as the outward trip. For all his giant strength, Lucas was tiring. The bitter cold had taken its toll of his resources, too. Toiling up the last few hundred yards of the climb to the vantage point in the gully overlooking the cave mouth, he was forced to halt for rest at shorter and shorter intervals. He arrived at last and sank down, dumping his burden in the snow.

It had been two hours since Lucas had left the spot, but the scene below was unchanged. The score or more Yraci still crouched waiting, outside the dark entrance to the cranny where the men had taken refuge. The darkness or the cold, it seemed, had the effect of reducing the activity of the aliens; there was no more nervous darting here and there, no fruitless exploration of routes up the slopes, no activity along the narrow trail. The besiegers seemed content to crouch motionless but for aimless waving of arms, and wait.

Wait for what? Lucas wondered. Maybe they're bringing up some big guns of their own. And if so, I'd better get moving. . . .

He righted the steering engine, placed it in a convenient crevice in an exposed rock slab, and packed snow around it, taking care to lead the control cables out into the clear. He aligned it carefully, then heaped other stones over it, packing the interstices with ice. In use, the engine was endothermic, absorbing heat from its surroundings. Firing it would freeze the entire mass into a single unit.

And now he was ready. Lying flat behind the improvised heat cannon, he grasped a wire in each hand, bringing them together—

A tremendous weight struck him in the back, slamming him against the heaped stones and ice around the engine, in the same instant that, with a hard, racking bellow, the engine burst into life. Lucas, half-stunned by the impact, twisted onto his back, fighting against the grasping, threshing bulk that had hurled itself on him so unexpectedly. He had a confused glimpse of a weird, triangular head, the scarred, horny thoracial plates and multijointed arms of a giant of the Yrax species; then the alien sprang clear, rearing up to bring its anterior limbs to bear. But Lucas was not the man to wait for the attack. He threw himself at the ungainly, ten-foot creature, knocked its rodlike legs from under it, grappled it around the body. Its limbs flashed as it struck vainly at him, but he rose to his knees, and using the full power of his giant torso and shoulders, hurled the alien from him. It raked at the ice, sending up a shower of chips; then it was gone, to slam down the steep slope with a crash like a ground car striking an abutment.

The roar of the steering engine had continued without pause. As Lucas clawed his way back to it, he saw at once that the impact of his body under the Yrax's attack had knocked it out of its careful alignment. The jet stream—a blue-white bar of ravening energy that lit the scene like a flare—instead of raking the besieging aliens, was searing the naked ice slope above the cave, sending a vast cloud of exploding steam boiling up against the sky. Vainly, the engineer threw his weight against the emplacement; but the engine was locked in a solid frozen matrix as impervious as granite.

As Lucas stared in bitter dismay at the target point across the gorge, the entire slope seemed to stir at once. With infinite leisure, cracks opened all across the great sheet of ice. Slabs the size of skating rinks came sliding down to spill over the edge and slam down on the ledge below. In moments, the hollow was a churning cauldron of whirling snow, driven up by the stream of snow, ice, and rock arriving in an ever-increasing volume from above. Here and there, around the periphery of the bowl-shaped space, a Yrax was visible, frantically attempting to climb the encircling wall, only to fall back and disappear in the blinding flurry.

Lucas found a loose fragment of stone, pounded at the ice encasing the bellowing engine, exposed the control wires. He ripped them apart and instantly the booming echoes crashed and died. The rumble and thud of falling ice dwindled, faded out. The blizzard driven up by the avalanche settled, revealing heaped banks from which here and there struggling alien limbs projected. But where the mouth of the cave had been, great drifts of broken ice rose up, burying it at least ten feet deep.

A lone Yrax freed itself from the snow, hurried to the point at which the trail had led from the hollow. But now a wall of snow barred egress. The alien scouted back and forth, tried to find a foothold, fell back, tried again, but fell back again. Others of the buried creatures were struggling clear of their icy entombment, and each tried and failed to find a route out of the hollow.

They're trapped, Lucas thought numbly. But so are Jim

and Wy. I could lead them out the back way—if I could reach it. They can't do it alone in the dark, even if Wy could carry Jim.

And even if they got clear—what then? We can't live long in this ice hell. . . .

There was a sound from below and behind Lucas. He crawled to the spot where he had thrust the giant alien over the edge. Twelve feet below, the alien crouched, its oddly featureless face turned up toward him. One of its legs was broken in two places.

"You're in a bad spot too, aren't you, fellow?" Lucas said aloud. "It looks like nobody wins and everybody loses."

A ratchety sound came from the creature below. Then a rasping voice which seemed to emanate from a point on the alien's back said clearly:

"Human, I underestimated you. It was a grave fault, and for that fault I die."

For a moment, Lucas was stunned into paralysis by the astonishing speech. But only for a moment.

"Where did you learn to speak Terran?" he said.

"For nine hundred ship periods I have monitored your transmissions of pictures and voices," the alien said in its flat, unaccented tone. "It was a strange phenomenon, worth investigation though passing understanding."

"Why haven't you communicated with us before?"

"For what purpose?"

"To end this tomfool war!" Lucas burst out. "What do you want from us? Why do you raid our colonies and attack our ships?"

The creature was silent for a long moment.

"It is the way of life," it said. "Could it be otherwise?"

"We could cooperate," Lucas said. "The galaxy is big enough for everybody."

"Cooperate? I know the word. It is a concept I have been unable to analyze."

"To work together. You help us, and we help you."

"But—how can this paradox be? Your survival and mine are mutually exclusive destiny-patterns. It is the nature of life for each being to strive to destroy all competitors."

"Is that why you've been killing men wherever you found them?"

"I have not tried to kill you," the Yrax stated. "Only your . . ." It used an incomprehensible word. Lucas asked for a translation.

"Your . . . cell bodies. Minions. Worker units. Curious—I cannot find the word in your tongue."

"You're not making sense. You were trying hard to kill us when you shot our boat down!"

"You speak as though . . . there were other men in association with you." The alien seemed deeply puzzled about something.

"It takes more than one man to operate even a scout boat. Anyway, a man would go crazy in space alone."

"You are saying that you *shared your ship with other men*?"

"Naturally."

"But—what kept you from tearing each other to pieces, as is the law of life?"

"If that's a law, it's time it was repealed," Lucas said. "Listen, Yrax—you're not making any sense. You had a crew of over twenty Yraci on your own ship—"

"Never! There was only I."

"You're talking nonsense, Yrax. A couple of dozen of

them are digging themselves out of the ice not fifty yards from here!"

"Those! But they are only my cell bodies, not Yraci!"

"They look exactly like you—"

"To alien sensors, perhaps—but they are no more than extensions of myself, spored off by me as needed, mindless creatures of my will. Surely, it is the same with you? I sensed, through their perceptors, that you, as I, are larger than your workers. Surely, the two units trapped in the cave are creatures of your mind and body, responsive to your thoughts, having no volition of their own? Can it be otherwise, in all sanity?"

"It is otherwise," Lucas said. "So you never heard of co-operation, eh? Well, you claim to have all the brains in your party. I have a proposition for you. . . ."

"I had to give him credit for seeing logic when it was pointed out to him," Lucas said forty-one hours later, seated before the alien control panel of the launch provided by the Yrax. "Without his crew men—or cell bodies, as he calls them—and I suppose he has a right to, his biology isn't much like ours— Without them, he was dead. When I told him I knew an escape route from the trap—and that I'd show it to him, if he'd lend us transport to get home—he agreed in a hurry."

"You took a chance, trusting him," Cameron said. "After you hauled him out and splinted his leg, he could have nipped you in two with those arms of his."

"He'd still have been stuck. He needed me to guide his boys out. Once he got the idea through his head that we could actually work together instead of automatically killing each other, things worked fine. It took us a few hours to melt a route to the top, and clear the cave mouth, and he did his share like a trooper."

"It's strange to think of a race of intelligent beings who never see each other, never have any contact, still developing a technology."

"With mutual telepathy, what any one of them learned, they all know. And they can create as many cell bodies as they need to do whatever they want done. I don't suppose there are more than a few hundred of the 'brain' Yraci on their planet—but there are millions of their workers."

"Not what you'd call a democracy," Wybold said.

"Their 'workers' are like our arms and legs," Lucas said. "Parts of their bodies. You couldn't very well give your fingers and toes an equal vote."

"Right now my stomach is giving the orders," Cameron said. "It says it's time to eat."

"Have a nutrient bar—courtesy of our Yrax friend," Lucas said. "They're not bad. Taste a little like stuffed dates. You know, there might be a market for them at home."

"The Yrax was pretty impressed by the energy-cell principle of the steering engine we gave him," Wybold said. "I foresee a brisk commerce between Terra and Yrax."

"It's a tragedy that there had to be all that destruction, ships blasted, lives lost—just because it never occurred to the Yraci to sit down and talk things over."

"It's not an easy lesson," Lucas said. "We humans had a little trouble learning it, if you remember your history." He grinned at Cameron, and the captain's black face grinned back at him.

Daughter

INTRODUCTION

Anne McCaffrey claims to be unique in the SF field, because she: was born on April 1, is "99 percent Irish," is a Radcliffe graduate, majored in Slavonic languages and literature. One could add that she is without question the best-known soprano in SF (her duets with tenor Isaac Asimov are legend), and she is a marvelous, exuberant, handsome woman.

But what really makes Anne McCaffrey unique is the kind of story that she writes. Stories that have won her the coveted Hugo Award of science fiction fandom and the Nebula Award of the Science Fiction Writers of America. Her novels include Dragonflight, The Ship Who Sang, Decision at Doona, Restoree, *and* Dragonquest. *She writes about dragons, singing spaceships, and the kind of girl who doesn't need Women's Lib because she's obviously talented, fast-thinking, and tough enough to stand up to whatever the wide universe can throw at her.*

"Daughter" is one of Anne McCaffrey's quieter stories, a thoughtful look at a not-too-distant future where people are still plagued by the unconscious, unthinking prejudices of those whom they love.

by ANNE McCAFFREY

THE moment her father began to yell at her twin brother Nick, Nora Fenn edged toward the door of the Complex office. George Fenn's anger always seemed to expand in direct proportion to the number of witnesses. She knew it humiliated Nick to be harangued in front of anyone, and this time there was absolutely nothing she could say in Nick's defense. Why hadn't he waited til she got back from school and could help him program the Planter?

"Fifty acres clearly marked corn," and Father stabbed a thick forefinger viciously at the corner of the room dominated by the scale model of the farm. He'd spent hours last winter rearranging the movable field units. In fact, Nora thought he displayed a lot more affectionate concern for the proper allocation of crops than he did for his two children. He certainly didn't berate the corn when the ears weren't plump or turned to ergot.

"And you," roared Father, suddenly clamping his hands tightly to his sides, as if he were afraid of the damage they'd do if he didn't, "*you* plant turnips. What kind of a programmer are you, Nicholas? A simple chore even your sister could do!"

Nora flinched at that. If Father ever found out that it was she, not Nick, who did the most complex programming . . .

She eased past the county maps, careful not to rustle the thin sheets of plastic overlay that Father had marked with crop, irrigation, and fertilizing patterns. The office was not small. One wall, of course, was the computer console and storage banks, then the window which looked out onto the big yard of the Complex, the three-foot-square relief model of the Fenn Farmlands on its stand. But two angry Fenns would diminish a Bargaining Hall.

Nora was struck by a resemblance between father and brother, which she'd not really appreciated before. Not only were both men holding their arms stiffly against their sides, but their jaws were set at the same obstinate angle, and each held one shoulder slightly higher than the other.

"I'm going to see that so-called Guidance Counselor of yours tomorrow and find out what kind of abortive computer courses you've been given. I thought I'd made it plain what electives you were to take."

"I get the courses I'm able to absorb. . . ."

Oh, please, Nick, breathed Nora, don't argue with him. The Educational Advancements will be posted in a day, two at the most, and then there's nothing he can do to alter the decision.

"Fenns are landsmen," Father shouted. "Born to the land, bred by the land. . . ."

The dictum reverberated through the room, and Nora used the noise to mask the slipping sound of the office door. She was out in the narrow passageway before Father realized that he'd lost part of his audience. She half ran to the outer door, the spongy-fiber flooring masking the sounds of her booted feet. When she was safely outside the rambling trilevel habitation, she breathed with relief. She'd better finish her own after-school chores. Now that Father'd got started on Nick, he'd be finding fault elsewhere. Since there weren't any apprentice landsmen on the Fenn Farm Complex right now, "elsewhere" could only be Nora. Mother never came in for Father's criticism, because everything she did in her quiet unspectacular way was done perfectly. Nora sighed. It wasn't fair to be so good at everything. Mary Fenn would laugh when her children complained and remarked that practice made perfect. But Mother always had some bit of praise, or a hug or a kiss to hearten you when she knew you'd *tried.* Father. . . . If Father would only say something encouraging to Nick . . .

Nora stayed to the left of the low, rambling, living quarters, out of the view angle from the office window. She glanced across the huge, plasti-cobbled yard which she had just finished hosing down. Yes, she had washed down the bay doors of the enormous barn which housed the Complex's Seeder, Plowboy, and Harvester. And done a thorough job of cleaning the tracks on which the heavy equipment was shunted out of the yard and onto the various rails leading to the arable tracts.

Turnips! If only Nick had blown the job with a high-priority vegetable, like beets or carrots. But turnips? They were nothing but subsistence level food. Father cannily complied with Farm Directives and still managed to plant most of Fenn lands to creditable crops like corn and beets. Fifty more acres of turnips this year might mean Nick would have that much less free credit at the university.

Nora sighed. Educational Advancements were only a day or so away. The suspense would be over, the pressure off the graduating students. Who'd go on to Applied and Academic Advancement in her class, she wondered? But there was no way of finding out short of stealing Counselor Fremmeng's wrist recorder. You only heard pass/fail decisions in elementary grades. An arbitrary percentile evaluation defeated the purpose of modern educational methods. Achievement must be measured by individual endeavor, not mean averages or sliding curves. Young citizens were taught to learn that knowledge was required of contributing citizens. Computer assisted drill constantly checked on comprehension of concept and use of basic skills. Educational Advancement, either Applied or Academic, depended as much on demonstrated diligence and application as inherent ability. Consequently, the slow student had every bit as much chance, and just as much right to education as the quick learner.

Well, Nora told herself briskly, it doesn't contribute anything to society to stand here daydreaming. You'll know in a day or two. In the meantime . . .

Nora went through the grape arbor toward the skimmer shed, at the far left by the compound wall. She had just turned in when she felt the reverberation of rapid thudding through the linked plasti-cobbles. Then Nick came pounding around the side of the building.

"Nora, lend me your skimmer?" he begged, unracking it as he spoke. "Mine's still drying out from Saturday's irrigating."

"But, Nick . . . Father . . ."

Nick's face darkened the way Father's did when he met resistance.

"Don't give me any static, Nor. I gotta change state. . . ."

"Oh, Nick, *why* didn't you wait until I could've checked you out?"

Nick set his jaw, his eyes blinking rapidly.

"You had to see Fremmeng, remember? And when I got home, the orders were waiting and I couldn't. I'm due over at Felicity's *now*." Nick turned up the pressure gauge, filling the tanks of the skimmer. "Orders. Orders. That's all I ever get from him. That and 'Fenns are crop farmers.' " Nick snorted. "He thinks he can program kids like a computer. Well, I'm *not* a crop farmer. It switches me off. Off!"

"Nick, please. Keep unity. Once you get to the university, *you* choose the courses you want. He can't go against Educational Advancement. And if he tries, you can always claim sanctuary against parental coercion. There isn't anyone in the Sector who wouldn't support your claim. . . ."

Nick was staring at her, incredulous, but suddenly the anger drained out of him, replaced by an exaggerated expression of tolerant forbearance.

"Claim sanctuary? I haven't lost all sense of unity, Nora," he told her sternly. "Hey, what did Fremmeng want to see *you* for?"

"Me? Oh, he had the absolutely most irrelevant questions! About how you and I get along, my opinions on family harmony and social contributions, and pairing off."

Nick regarded her with an intent, impersonal stare.

"He did, huh? Look, Nor," and her brother's mood changed state completely, "I need to see Felicity. I gotta blow out of *here*!"

Nora grabbed at his arm as he inflated the skimmer.

"Nick, what *did* you say to Father?"

Nick gave her a sour look now. "I told him he'd better hold off making so many big plans for me to be the Fenn Complex's Master Ruralist, until he sees the Educational Advancements."

"Nick, if you don't get Advancement, Father will just . . . just . . ."

"Abort and sulk!" Nick finished for her. "No, I'll get Advancement, all right. On my terms! There's not a blasted thing wrong with Applied. It's Father who tried programming the university for me. But I've had different plans." Nick's look turned as hard as Father's could when he'd lost crop.

"What do you mean, Nick? What have you been doing?" Nora was suddenly scared. What had Father driven Nick to do?

"Nora, sweetie, Old Bates at the Everett Complex is about due for retirement. Felicity Everett and I want to pair off as soon as the E.A.s have been posted. And it's just possible that Landsman Everett would opt for me as assistant." Nick's expression altered again, this time to enthusiasm, and Nora felt relief at the change.

"Oh, he would, Nick. You know what he said about your term paper on ovine gene manipulation." Then Nora caught the significance of his plan.

"Yes, indeedy, sister mine. Nick can cut a program on his own, without yours or Father's help."

She was so astonished at the calculation in his smile that he was able to loosen her fingers from the handlebars. He was off on the skimmer at a high blow before she could stop him.

"Nick . . ."

"Give my love to our foul-feathered friends!" he called over his shoulder cheerfully, and launched the skimmer straight across the meadows toward the Everetts' Herd Complex.

Resolutely, Nora made for the distant Poultry house on

foot. She hated this chore and usually swapped it with Nick. Father proclaimed that chickens and turkeys were a woman's business. Nick found poultry a trifle more engrossing than the tedious crop programming.

Why couldn't Nick have put a little more attention on what he was doing instead of expending all his energies thwarting Father? Irritably, she scuffed at a vagrant pebble in the track which led straight from the low-rambling Farm Complex, set in the fold of the soft hills, toward the Poultry house. She could see the glitter of the round roof as she topped the next rise.

Educational Advancement! She so hoped that she'd qualify . . . at least for Applied Advancement. That would prove to Father she wasn't all that stupid, even if she was a girl. Maybe, if she could make Journeyman Class Computer . . . she really felt that she understood mathematics and logistics. . . . But if she got Journeyman, Father mightn't be so disappointed when he finally realized that Nick was so absolutely set against crop farming. While Father might feel that women were educated far beyond society's profit, no contributing citizen could argue with the Advancement Board's decision. For they were impartial, having the best interests of society *and* the individual. Father might scoff at the premise that everyone had the constitutional right to shelter, food, clothing, *and* education as long as he maintained a class average. But then, Father disparaged a system which rewarded the diligent student with credit bonuses for something as intangible as academic excellence.

"That doesn't feed anyone, make anything, buy or sell anything," he'd say when he'd started on that tangent. There was no use explaining to such a pragmatist.

If Nora could get certified in computer logistics and was able to handle the Complex's Master Ruralist, then surely he'd be proud of her. He wouldn't mind that his other child had been a girl, not the second boy *he'd* printed into the Propagation Registration.

Father never let Nora, or her mother, forget that he had not computed twins, nor mixed sexes. *He'd* opted for both legal progeny to be male. Since early sex education in school, Nora had wondered how her mother had managed not only a multiple birth but a split in sexes without Father's knowledge. For one thing, multiple births had been uncommon for the last hundred years, since Population Control had been initiated. Most duly registered couples opted for one of each sex, well spaced. Of course, George Fenn would complain about PC, too. Or rather, the provision which permitted only exceptional couples—in return for extraordinary contributions to society—to have one or two more children above the legal number.

"They put the emphasis on the wrong genetic factors," Father would argue bitterly whenever the subject came up. "If you breed for brain, the species weakens physically, flaws develop." He'd always flex his huge biceps then, show off his two-meter-tall, one-hundred-kilo frame as a fine case in point of his argument. He'd been disappointed, too, when Nick, scarcely an undersized man, stopped slightly short of two meters in height. Father'd glower at Nora, as if her slender body had robbed her twin of extra centimeters.

How had Mary Fenn, a woman of muted qualities, coped so long and amiably with her husband? Her quiet, uncritical voice was seldom raised. She knew when you were upset, though, or sick, and her capable hands were sure and soft. If anyone deserved Maternity Surplus, it was mother. She was so good! She even managed to remain completely in control of herself, a presence unperturbed by her husband's tirades and intemperate attitudes, efficiently dealing with each season and its exigencies.

Of course, it was no wonder that Mother was quiet. Father was such a dominating person. He could shout down an entire Rural Sector Meeting.

"A fine landsman," Nora heard her father called. "But don't cross him," she'd heard whispered. "He'll try to program things his way, come hell or high water. He knows the land, though," was the grudging summation.

"Knows the land, but not humans," Nora muttered under her breath. "Not his children. Certainly he doesn't know what his son really wants."

Maybe once Nick gets away to the university, harmony would be restored between father and son. Nick ought to have more desire to keep family unity. . . .

Crop farming wasn't all that bad, Nora thought. Now you could mow a thousand-acre field, as Nora had done as a preteen when the apprentices let her, by punching the right buttons. You could winnow and cull with a vacuum attachment; grade, bag, clean your field far more efficiently than the most careful ancient gleaners. You could program your Plowboy to fertilize at five levels as the seed was planted. One Complex with two families or a couple of responsible apprentices could efficiently farm an old-time, county-sized spread and still turn a luxury credit. Not to mention having fresh and ready supplies of any edible and some of those luxuries the City Complexes craved above the subsistence level.

Now Nora could hear the muted pitiful honking of the geese in the Poultry house. She winced. There were certain aspects of farming that could not be completely automated. You can't tape a broody hen, and you can't computerize the services of a rooster. Cocks' crows still heralded sunrise over the fields, whether the clarion summons issued from a wooden slated crate or the sleek multipentangle that housed the feathered varieties raised by the Fenn Complex. Eggs laid by the hens in Nora's charge would be powdered and eventually whipped to edibility on the Jupiter station, or be flash-frozen to provide sustenance when the first colony ship set forth as it was rumored to do in the next decade. Turkeys from this Complex regularly made the one-way trip to the Moon bases for Winter Solstice celebrations, call them Saturnalias or Santa Claus if you would.

She entered the poultry pentangle through the access tunnel straight to the computer core which handled all watering, feeding, cleaning, egg collection, and slaughter operations. The Fenn Complex did not sell to dietary groups, so the market preparations were the standard ones.

She checked the tapes on the Leghorn fifth, replenished the grit supply, and tapped out a reorder sequence. She flushed out all the pen floors and refreshed the water. Then she checked the mean weight of the tom turkeys, growing from scrawny, long-legged adolescence to plump-breasted tail fanners. A trifle more sand for digestion, a richer mash for firmer meats, and a little less of the growth hormones. Concentrated goodness, not size for size's sake anymore.

The geese were fattening, too, on their fixed perches. Goose livers on the rod. Nora hated the calculated cruelty that brought in credit margin for the Fenn Complex. Stuff the poor helpless fowl, engorge their livers for the delectation of the gourmet. The geese lived sheltered, circumscribed lives, which was not living at all, for they couldn't see out of their own quarters. Nothing distracted them from their purpose in life—death from enlarged livers. Nora was distracted from her chore by the shrill note of their honking. She forced herself to read the gauges. Yes, the upper group were ready for market. Even their plaint registered the truth of their self-destruction. They'd been bred for one purpose. It was their time to fulfill it. She coldly dialed for a quotation on the price of goose and goose liver at the Central Farm Exchange. The European price printed out at a respectable high. She routed the information to the Farm's main console. It might just sweeten Father's mood to realize a quick credit on the sale. She sure didn't look forward to the rest of the day, if nothing leavened his cantankerous mood.

Nora took a detour on the way back, across the one-hundred-acre field. The willows which her great-grandfather had planted the day the Farm Reforms were passed were tipped with raw yellow. Spring was an Earth-moment away. Soon the golden limbs would sprout their green filaments, to drape and float them on the irrigation ditch which watered their thirsty feet. Would *her* great-grandchildren admire the willows in their turn? The whimsy irritated her. How dared she determine what her great-grandchildren might do?

She walked faster, away from what the willows stood for. She didn't really have to be back at the Complex until mealtime, an hour or so away. Father always programmed too much time for her to tend the Poultry house, an unflattering assessment of her ability, but usually that had given her more time for something she'd wanted to do which Father might not approve of as contributory. If only *once* he'd look at her as if she weren't something that had got printed out by mistake. How in the name of little printed circuits *had* Mother dared to have twins?

Nora used her spare time to pick cress at the sluice gate beds. It was a soothing occupation and contributed toward dinner's salad. When she finally got back to the house, she glanced into the office. The print-out slot was clear, so Father had seen her report. She'd simply have to wait to find out if he'd acted on the data. The main console was keyed to his code only.

She heard the meal chime from the kitchen area and quickly brought the cress out to her mother, who was taking roast lamb out of the oven. Did Mother know about Nick's quarrel? Lamb was her father's favorite protein.

"Oh, cress! That was a considerate thought, Nora. We'll put a few sprigs on the lamb platter for looks. There'll only be three of us for dinner, you know."

Nora didn't know, for surely Nick would be back from the Everett Complex; but just then Father came in, grim-faced, and sat down. Again Nora wondered just how far he had goaded Nick this afternoon. Why had she played the coward and left?

The tender lamb stuck in her throat like so much dry feed. Her stomach seemed to close up as if eating had been programmed out, but she forced herself to clear her plate. No one, in this day and age and especially at George Fenn's table, wasted real food. Once, as a child—but only that once—she had left real food on her plate. She'd spent the next two weeks trying to swallow common subsistence level rations.

Conversation was never encouraged at Fenn meals, so the awkward meal never seemed to end. When Nora could finally excuse herself and make for the sanctuary of her room, her father stopped her.

"So, Nora, you've been doing Nicholas' programming for him, eh?" Father's voice was icy with disapproval and his eyes hard specks of gray.

Nora stared back, speechless. Oh, Nick couldn't have!

"Don't gawk at me, girl. Answer!" Father's big fist banged the table and startled a "Yes, Father," from her.

"And how long has this . . . this deception gone on?"

Nora didn't dare look at him.

"How long?" Father repeated, his voice rising in volume and getting sharper.

"Since—since spring," she answered.

"*Which* spring?" was the acid query.

Nora swallowed hard, against the sudden nauseating taste of lamb in her mouth.

"The first year of programming."

"You *dared* take over a task assigned your brother—by me? Designed to acquaint him with the problems he'll face as a landsman?"

Instinctively, Nora leaned as far back in her chair, away from her father's looming body, as she could. Not even George Fenn would disrupt family harmony by striking a child, but he was so angry that it seemed to Nora he was some terrible stranger, capable even of physical indignity.

"Nick couldn't seem to get the trick of it," she managed to say in her own defense. "I only helped a little. When he got jammed."

"He's a Fenn. He's got farming in his blood. Five generations of farming. You've robbed him of his heritage, of his proper contribution . . ."

"Oh, no, Father. Nick's always contributed. He'd do the Poultry . . ." and her sentence broke off as she saw the bloated, red face of her father.

"You dared . . . *dared* swap assignments?"

"You miss the point entirely, George," Mother interceded in her placid way. "The tasks were completed, were well done, so I cannot see why it is so wrong for Nick to have done which and Nora, what. They're both Fenns, after all. That's the core of the matter."

"Have you changed state, woman?" Father wanted to know, but astonishment had aborted his anger. "Nicholas is my son! Nora's only a girl."

"Really, George. Don't quibble. You know, I've been thinking of enlarging my contribution to society now that the children are about to advance. I'd really like to go back to the Agriculture Institute and update my credentials. Sometimes," Mother went on in the conversational way in which she was apt to deliver startling conclusions, "I think the children have studied a whole new language when I hear them discussing computer logistics. Remember when I used to take an apprentice's place, George? Of course, it would be much more interesting for me if you'd diversify the Complex. I can't have any more children, of course, but if we bred lambs or calves, I'd've young things to tend again. Society does say it'll satisfy every individual's needs." She gave her husband an appealing smile. "Do try to compute that in your fall program, George. I'd appreciate it."

Looking at Mother as if she'd taken leave of her senses, Father rose and pushed back his chair. He mumbled something about checking urgent data but stumbled out of the dining area, past the office, and out of the house.

"Mother, I'd no idea . . ."

The rest of Nora's words died in her throat because her mother looked about to laugh, her eyes beaming with mischief.

"I oughtn't to do that to George when he's had a big dinner. But there're more ways to kill a cat than choking him with butter—as my grandmother used to say. Although that's a shocking way to use butter—not to mention a good cat—but Grandmother was full of such dairy-oriented expressions. Hmmm. Now dairy farming might not be such a bad compromise, considering the print-out quotes on milk and cheese this spring." Then she closed her lips firmly as if her own loquacity startled her as much as it did Nora. The laughter died in her eyes. "Nora?"

"Yes, Mother?"

"In this society, a person is legally permitted to develop at his own pace and follow his own aptitudes. Not even a stubborn atavist like your father has the right to inhibit another's contribution. Of course, the responsible citizen tries to maintain harmonious relations with his family unit up to that point of interference.

"You realize, I'm certain, that even if Nick has no love of crop farming, he is basically attuned to rural life. I've been so grateful to you, dear, for . . . soothing matters between your father and brother." The words came out haltingly and Mother didn't look directly at her, but Nora could appreciate her difficulty. Mother had scrupulously avoided taking sides in the constant interchanges between Nick and Father. She had somehow always maintained family unity. Her unexpected frankness was essentially a betrayal of that careful neutrality. "I had hoped that Nick might be a more biddable boy, able to go along with his father's ambitions. They may be old-fashioned . . ."

"Mother, you *know* Father is positively medieval at times." Nora regretted her flippancy when she saw the plea for understanding in her mother's eyes. "Well, he is, but that's his bit. And he does make a distinguished contribution as a landsman."

"Yes, Nora. Few men these days have your father's real love of the earth. It isn't every landsman," Mother added, her voice proud, "who runs a Complex as big as ours and makes a creditable balance."

"If only Father didn't *try* . . ."

But Mother was looking off into the middle distance, her face so troubled, her eyes dark with worry, that Nora wanted to cry out that she really did understand. Hadn't she proved that with all she'd done to keep unity?

"You're a kind, thoughtful, considerate child, Nora," Mother said finally, smiling with unexpected tenderness. "You undoubtedly rate very high on interpersonal relationships. . . ."

"You must, too," Nora protested, glancing toward the office.

Mother gave a little rueful laugh. "I do, or I shouldn't have got on so well with your father all these years. But, right now, we both have to work together to maintain family harmony."

"You haven't had a deficiency notice on me, have you?"

"Good lands, no, child," and Mother was clearly startled at the notion. "But Nick had an interview with Counselor Fremmeng and he's reasonably certain, from the way the Counselor talked, that he is going to disappoint your father. You know that George has been positive Nick would receive Academic Advancement. And frankly, Nora, Nick not only doesn't want it, he's sure he won't get it."

"Yes, he mentioned something like that to me this afternoon after Father reamed him," Nora said sadly. "But what could Father possibly do in the face of E.A. postings except admit that he couldn't compute Nick into his own program?"

Mother gave Nora one of her long disconcertingly candid stares.

"It's not a question, Nora, of what your Father would or would not do. It's a question of how we maintain family unity and your father's dignity and standing in the Sector. With a little tactful and affectionate . . . handling . . . he can think it was all his own notion in the first place."

Nora stared at her mother with dawning and respectful admiration.

"That's why you offered to update your credentials?"

Mother grinned. "Just thought I'd plant the notion. It *is* spring, you know."

"Mother, why on earth did you marry Father?" Nora asked in a rush. She might never get another chance to find out.

An unexpectedly tender expression on her mother's face made her appear younger, prettier.

"Land's sake, because he was the kind of man I wanted to marry," Mary Fenn said with a proud lift of her chin. "A man to do for, and George takes a lot of doing, you know. Keeps me on my toes. He has such tremendous vitality. I like that. He knows and loves and understands the land, and I wanted that, too. I knew that was good for me, to be close to the land, and I wanted to raise my children close to natural things. Sometimes I think there's too much dependence on technology. I'm a throwback, too, Nora, just as much as your father is with his antiquated notions of a son following in his father's footsteps on land that's been in the same family for generations." Mother looked down at her square-palmed, strong-fingered hands as if they represented her inner self. "I like to feel warm earth, to get dirty. I want *to do* with my hands, not just let them idly punch a button or two. I like growing things, young things. If I could've defied the Population Control laws, too, I'd've had a whole passel of brats to raise. As it was . . ." and the softness became a glowing smile of love and compassion that could encompass the whole county.

"As it was," Nora said with a giggle, "you had twins in spite of Father."

"Yes," Mary Fenn chuckled, her eyes alit with laughter, "I had twins. A boy for your father," and her face was both dutiful and mischievous, "and a girl for me."

"Well, Nick's not the son Father wanted. Mother—" and suddenly the answer was the most important thing in Nora's life, "Mother, am I the daughter *you* wanted?"

The laughter died abruptly and Mother placed her square hands on either side of Nora's face.

"You're a good child, Nora. You never complain. You work hard and willingly. Yes, you're a good daughter."

But that wasn't the answer Nora wanted.

"But what do *you* want me to *be*?"

"Happy, Nora. I want you to be happy." Mary Fenn turned, then, to glance around the kitchen area, checking to see if all were in order. It was a dismissal, a tacit gesture not to pursue this subject further. Her mother often did that. Particularly with Father. She didn't actually evade a question, simply didn't answer it directly or fully.

"Mother, that isn't enough of an answer anymore."

Her mother turned back to her, her eyebrows raised in a

polite question which turned to a frown when she'd studied her daughter's stern face.

"I only wanted a daughter, Nora, not a child in my own image, to follow in my path. Just a girl child to raise, to love, to delight in. A woman is proud to bear her son, but she rejoices in her daughter. You've given me much secret joy, Nora. I'm proud of you for many, silly little motherly reasons you'll understand when you have your own daughter. Beyond that . . ." Mother began to move away. "I believe that everyone must be allowed to determine his own life's course. In that respect I am completely modern. Do *you* dislike farm life as much as your brother, Nora?"

"No," but Nora realized as she said it that she was no longer sure. "It's not that I dislike it, Mother, it's just that I'd prefer to do something more . . ."

"More cerebral, less manual?" her mother asked teasingly.

Nora could feel the blush mounting in her cheeks. She didn't want Mother to think she felt farming wasn't a substantial contribution.

"Well," and her mother's voice was brisk again, "the Advancements will soon be posted. They'll decide the matter once and for all. In the meantime . . ."

"I'll be a good daughter."

"I know I can count on you," and there was a sudden worried edge to her mother's voice. "Now go. You've studying, I know. You want to achieve a good credit bonus at graduation."

Nora let her mother's gentle shove propel her toward the ramp up to the bedroom level. But she was far too disquieted to study. Her mother had never been so forthright, and yet Nora did not feel the reassurance which ought to have resulted from such frankness.

There'd been many nuances in the conversation, emotional overtones which her mother had never permitted her daughter to hear before. And so many shifts. Almost as if Mother had really been sounding her out. On what? Useless to examine emotions: they were too subjective. They weren't computable data.

Nora tapped out a request for a mathematics review, senior level, on her home-study console. She was still staring at the first problem, when the computer pinged warningly and then chattered out the answer. Nora turned off the console and sat staring at the printout.

Was she really the daughter Mary Fenn had wanted? How would she ever know? She was certainly not the second son her father had intended to sire, though she had all the capabilities he'd wanted. If Nick wouldn't crop farm the Fenn Complex, how were they going to get Father to accept a compromise? Maybe Mother wanted her to prove to Father that she knew more about crop farming than Nick right now? No, George Fenn wanted his *son* to follow him at Fenn Complex. If not Nick, then some man, because George Fenn's atavistic temperament required him to pass land on to a man, not a woman, even of his own genetic heritage.

This year's apprentices would be assigned here soon, fresh from their courses in Applied Agriculture at the Institute. Maybe she'd like one of them, pair off with him, and then the Fenn land would at least remain in partially Fenn hands for another generation. Was this what Mother had been hinting at when she mentioned Nora's rating in IPR?

No, the trick would be to get Father to agree to diversify. That way Nick, who was just as stubborn as his father, could follow his heart's desire, and society would benefit all around. But, when Mother brought that notion up at mealtime, Father had rushed out of the house as if his circuits had jammed.

Nora looked disconsolately down at the console. Computers reacted within the parameters of the programming, to taped instructions, facts that could be ineradicably stored on minute bits. Only humans put no parameters on dreams and stored aspirations.

The sound of a vehicle braking to a stop broke into her thoughts. Nick had come back!

The angle of the house was such that Nora could only see the blunt anonymous end of a triwheel from her window. Nick had her skimmer. But—Nora grasped at the notion—Nick had gone to the Everetts! Maybe Landsman Everett was bringing him back. Father openly admired the breeder, said he was a sound husbandman and made a real contribution to society.

Nora sat very still, straining to hear Nick's voice or Landsman Everett's cheerful tenor. She heard only the subdued murmur of her mother's greeting, and then Father's curt baritone. When she caught a second deep male rumble, she ceased listening and turned back to the console. She did have exams to pass, and eavesdropping did not add to family unity.

Nora usually enjoyed computer assisted drill. It put one on the mental alert. She enjoyed the challenge of completing drill well within the allotted time. So, despite her concerns, she was soon caught up by study habits. She finished the final level of review with only one equation wrong. Her own fault. She'd skipped a step in her hurry to beat the computer's time. She never could understand why some kids said they were exhausted after a computer assisted session. She always felt great.

"Nora!"

Her father's summons startled her. Had she missed his first call? He sounded angry. You never made Father call you twice.

"Coming!" Anxious not to irritate him, she ran down the ramp to the lower level, apologizing all the way. "Sorry, Father, I was concentrating on CAI review . . ." and then she saw that the visitor was Counselor Fremmeng. She muttered a nervous good evening. This was the time of year for Parent Consultations, and deficiencies were usually scheduled first. She couldn't have made that poor a showing. . . . A glance at her father's livid face told her that this interview was not going the way George Fenn wanted it.

"Counselor Fremmeng has informed me that *you* have achieved sufficient distinction in your schooling to warrant Academic Advancement."

The savage way her father bit the words out, the disappointment written on his face dried up any thought Nora had of exulting in her achievement. Hurt and bewildered, unaccountably rebuked in yet another effort to win his approval, Nora stared back at him. Even if she was a girl, surely he didn't hate her for getting Academic. . . . In a sudden change of state, she realized why.

"Then Nick didn't?"

Her father turned from her coldly so that Counselor Fremmeng had to confirm it. His eyes were almost sad in his long, jowled face. Didn't *he* take pride in her achievement? Didn't anyone? Crushed with disappointment, Nora pivoted slowly, and when she met her mother's eyes saw in them something greater than mere approval, an expectation, an entreaty. "Your brother," Father went on with such scathing bitterness that Nora shuddered, "has been *tentatively* allowed two years of Applied Advancement. The wisdom of society has limited this to the Agricultural Institute with the recommendation that he study *animal husbandry.*" He turned back to face his daughter, eyes burning, huge frame rigid with emotion.

Serves him right, Nora thought and aborted such disrespect. He had been too certain that Nick would qualify for the university and become a Computer Master for the Fenn Complex. He'll just have to adjust. A Fenn is going on. Me.

"How . . ." and suddenly George Fenn erupted, seeking relief from his disappointment with violent pacing and exaggerated gestures of his huge hands, "how can a girl qualify when her brother, of the same parentage, raised in the same environment, given the same education at the same institution, receives only a tentative acceptance? Tentative! Why, Nicholas has twice the brains his sister has!"

"Not demonstrably, Landsman," Counselor Fremmeng remarked, flicking a cryptic glance at Nora. "And certainly not the same intense application. Nick showed the most interest and diligence in biology and ecology. His term paper, an optional project on the mutation of angoran ovines, demonstrated an in-depth appreciation of genetic manipulation. Society encourages such . . ."

"But sheep!" Father interrupted him. "Fenns are crop farmers."

"A little diversity improves any operation," Counselor Fremmeng said with such uncharacteristic speciousness that Nora stared at him.

"My son may study sheep. Well then, what area of concentration has been opened to my . . . my daughter?"

Nora swallowed hard, wishing so much that Father would not look at her as if she'd been printed out by mistake. Then she realized the counselor was looking at *her* to answer her father.

"I'd prefer to . . ."

"What area is she qualified to pursue?" Father cut her off peremptorily, directing his question again to the counselor.

The man cleared his throat as he flipped open the wrist recorder and made an adjustment. He studied the frame for a long moment. It gave Nora a chance to assort her own thoughts. She really hadn't believed Nick this afternoon when he intimated he'd thwarted Father's plans. And she'd certainly never expected *Academic.*

The counselor tapped the side of the recorder thoughtfully, pursing his lips as he'd a habit of doing, Nora knew, when he was trying to phrase a motivating reprimand to an underachiever.

"Nora is unusually astute in mathematics and logistics. . . ." The counselor's eyes slid across her face, again that oblique warning. "She has shown some marked skill in Computer Design, but in order to achieve Computer Technician . . ."

"Computer Tech. . . . Could she actually make Technician status?" Father demanded sharply, and Nora could sense the change in him.

Counselor Fremmeng coughed suddenly, covering his mouth politely. When he looked up again, Nora could almost swear he'd been covering a laugh, not a cough. His little eyes were very bright. None of the other kids believed her when she said that the counselor was actually human, with a sense of humor. Of course, a man in his position had to maintain dignity in front of the student body.

"I believe that is quite within her capability, Landsman," Counselor Fremmeng said in a rather strained voice.

"Didn't you say, Counselor, that Nora qualified for unlimited Academic Advancement?" Mother asked quietly. She held Nora's eyes steadily for a moment before she turned with a little smile to her husband. "So, a Fenn *is* going on to the university this generation, just as you'd hoped, George. Now, if you could see your way clear to diversify. . . . And did you notice the premium angora fleece is bringing? You know how I've wanted young things to tend and lambs are so endearing. Why, I might even get Counselor Fremmeng to recommend updating for me at the Institute. Then, George, you wouldn't need to spend all those credits for apprentices. The Fenns could work the Complex all by themselves. Just like the old days!"

"It's an encouraging thing for me to have such a contributing family unit in my Sector. A real pleasure," Counselor said, smiling at the older Fenns before he gave Nora a barely perceptible nod.

"Well, girl, so you'll study Computology at the university?" asked Father. His joviality was a little forced, although his eyes were still cold.

"I ought to take courses in Stability Phenomena, Feedback Control, more Disturbance Dynamics . . ."

"Listen to the child. You'd never think such terms would come so easily to a girl's lips, would you?"

"Mathematics is scarcely a male prerogative, Landsman," said Counselor Fremmeng, rising. "It's the major tool of our present, sane, social structure. That and social dynamics.

Nora's distinguished herself in social psychology which is, as you know, the prerequisite for building the solid familial relationships which constitute the firm foundation of our society."

"Oh, she'll be a good mother in her time," Father said, still with that horrible edge to his heartiness. His glance lingered on his wife.

"Undoubtedly," the counselor agreed blandly. "However, there's more to maintaining a sound family structure than maternity. As Nora has demonstrated. If you'll come to my office after your exams on Thursday, Nora, we'll discuss your program at the university in depth, according to your potentials." His slight emphasis on the pronoun went unnoticed by George Fenn. Then the counselor bowed formally to her parents, congratulated them again on the achievements of their children, their contribution to society, and left.

"So, girl," said her father in a heavy tone, "*you'll* be the crop farmer in this generation!"

Nora faced him, unable to perjure herself. With his pitiful honking about farming Fenns, he was like the geese, fattening for their own destruction. She felt pity for him because he couldn't see beyond his perch on these acres. But he was doing what he'd been set in this life to do, as the geese were achieving their contribution to society, too.

Unlimited Academic Advancement! She'd never anticipated that. But she could see that it was in great measure due to her father. Because he had considered her inferior to Nick, she'd worked doubly hard, trying to win his approval. She realized now that she'd never have it, Father being what he was. And being the person she was, she'd not leave him in discord. She'd help maintain family unity until Father came to accept Nick as a sheep-breeder, diversification on the Fenn acres, a Fenn daughter in the university. Mother would step in to help with crop farming and there'd be no decrease in contribution.

"I'll do all I can to help you, Father," Nora said finally, realizing that her parents were waiting for her answer.

Then she caught her mother's shining eyes, saw in them the approval, the assurance she wanted. She knew she was the daughter her mother had wanted. *That* made her happy.

Something Wild Is Loose

INTRODUCTION

Robert Silverberg might well be what every little boy wants to become when he grows up: a gifted and hugely successful writer, urbane, witty, cool, married to a beautiful and brainy Ph.D., the recipient of science fiction's highest honors and awards. Who could ask for anything more?

How does he do it? He was born in New York and still lives there, in the former home of the late Mayor Fiorello La Guardia. He received a bachelor of arts degree from Columbia University. He travels a lot. He works even more. His books include nonfiction works such as The Man Who Found Nineveh *and* Lost Cities and Vanished Civilizations, *and SF novels such as* The Gate of Worlds, To Live Again, Tower of Glass, *and many, many others.*

In "Something Wild Is Loose," he takes a familiar SF subject—the alien among us—and turns it into a winning story about several marvelous people, one of whom isn't human.

by ROBERT SILVERBERG

THE Vsiir got aboard the Earthbound ship by accident. It had absolutely no plans for taking a holiday on a wet, grimy planet like Earth. But it was in its metamorphic phase, undergoing the period of undisciplined change that began as winter came on, and it had shifted so far up-spectrum that Earthborn eyes couldn't see it. Oh, a really skilled observer might notice a slippery little purple flicker once in a while, a kind of snore, as the Vsiir momentarily dropped down out of the ultraviolet; but he'd have to know where to look, and when.

The crew man who was responsible for putting the Vsiir on the ship never even considered the possibility that there might be something invisible sleeping atop one of the crates of cargo being hoisted into the ship's hold. He simply went down the row, slapping a floater node on each crate, and sending it gliding up the gravity well toward the open hatch. The fifth crate to go inside was the one on which the Vsiir had decided to take its nap. The spaceman didn't know that he had inadvertently given an alien organism a free ride to Earth. The Vsiir didn't know it, either, until the hatch was sealed and an oxygen-nitrogen atmosphere began to hiss from the vents. The Vsiir did not happen to breathe those gases, but, because it was in its time of metamorphosis, it was able to adapt itself quickly and nicely to the sour, prickly vapors seeping into its metabolic cells. The next step was to fashion a set of full-spectrum scanners and learn something about its surroundings. Within a few minutes, the Vsiir was aware—

—that it was in a large, dark place that held a great many boxes containing various mineral and vegetable products of its world, mainly branches of the greenfire tree but also some other things of no comprehensible value to a Vsiir—

—that a double wall of curved metal enclosed this place—

—that just beyond this wall was a null-atmosphere zone, such as is found between one planet and another—

—that this entire closed system was undergoing acceleration—

—that this therefore was a spaceship, heading rapidly away from the world of Vsiirs and in fact already some ten planetary diameters distant, with the gap growing alarmingly moment by moment—

—that it would be impossible, even for a Vsiir in metamorphosis, to escape from the spaceship at this point—

—and that, unless it could persuade the crew of the ship to halt and go back, it would be compelled to undertake a long and dreary voyage to a strange and probably loathsome world, where life would at best be highly inconvenient, and might present great dangers. It would find itself cut off painfully from the rhythm of its own civilization. It would miss the Festival of Changing. It would miss the Holy Eclipse. It would not be able to take part in next spring's Rising of the Sea. It would suffer in a thousand ways.

There were six human beings aboard the ship. Extending its perceptors, the Vsiir tried to reach their minds. Though humans had been coming to its planet for many years, it had never bothered making contact with them before; but it had never been in this much trouble before, either. It sent a foggy tendril of thought roving the corridors, looking for traces of human intelligence. Here? A glow of electrical activity within a sphere of bone: a mind, a mind! A busy mind. But surrounded by a wall, apparently; the Vsiir rammed up against it and was thrust back. That was startling and disturbing. What kind of beings were these, whose minds were closed to ordinary contact?

The Vsiir went on, hunting through the ship. Another mind: again closed. Another. And another. The Vsiir felt panic rising. Its mantle fluttered; its energy radiations dropped far down into the visible spectrum, then shot nervously toward much shorter waves. Even its physical form experienced a series of quick involuntary metamorphoses, to the Vsiir's intense embarrassment. It did not get control of its body until it had passed from spherical to cubical to chaotic, and had become a gridwork of fibrous threads held together only by a pulsing strand of ego. Fiercely, it forced itself back to the spherical form and resumed its search of the ship, dismally realizing that by this time its native world was half a stellar unit away. It was without hope now, but it continued to probe the minds of the crew, if only for the sake of thoroughness. Even if it made contact, though, how could it communicate the nature of its plight, and even if it communicated, why would the humans be disposed to help it? Yet it went on through the ship. And—

Here: an open mind. No wall at all. A miracle! The Vsiir rushed into close contact, overcome with joy and surprise, pouring out its predicament. —*Please listen. Unfortunate nonhuman organism accidentally transported into this ves-*

sel during loading of cargo. Metabolically and psychologically unsuited for prolonged life on Earth. Begs pardon for inconvenience; wishes prompt return to home planet left recently; regrets disturbance in shipping schedule, but hopes that this large favor will not prove impossible to grant. Do you comprehend my sending? Unfortunate nonhuman organism accidentally transported—

Lieutenant Falkirk had drawn the first sleep shift after float-off. It was only fair; Falkirk had knocked himself out processing the cargo during the loading stage, slapping the floater nodes on every crate, and feeding the transit manifests to the computer. Now that the ship was spaceborne, he could grab some rest while the other crew men were handling the float-off chores. So he settled down for six hours in the cradle as soon as they were on their way. Below him, the ship's six gravity drinkers spun on their axes, gobbling inertia and pushing up the acceleration, and the ship floated Earthward at a velocity that would reach the galactic level before Falkirk woke. He drifted into drowsiness. A good trip: enough greenfire bark in the hold to see Earth through a dozen fits of the molecule plague, and plenty of other potential medicinals besides, along with a load of interesting mineral samples, and— Falkirk slept. For half an hour he enjoyed sweet slumber, his mind disengaged, his body loose.

Until a dark dream bubbled through his skull.

Deep purple sunlight, hot and somber. Something slippery tickling the edges of his brain. He lies on a broad white slab in a scorched desert. Unable to move. Getting harder to breathe. The gravity—a terrible pull, bending and breaking him, ripping his bones apart. Hooded figures moving around him, pointing, laughing, exchanging blurred comments in an unknown language. His skin melting and taking on a new texture: porcupine quills sprouting inside his flesh and forcing their way upward, poking out through every pore. Points of fire all over him. A thin scarlet hand, withered fingers like crab claws, hovering in front of his face. Scratching. Scratching. Scratching. His blood running among the quills, thick and sluggish. He shivers, struggling to sit up—lifts a hand, leaving pieces of quivering flesh stuck to the slab—sits up—

He wakes, trembling, screaming.

Falkirk's shout still sounded in his own ears as his eyes adjusted to the light. Lieutenant Commander Rodriguez was holding his shoulders and shaking him.

"You all right?"

Falkirk tried to reply. Words wouldn't come. Hallucinatory shock, he realized, as part of his mind attempted to convince the other part that the dream was over. He was trained to handle crises; he ran through a quick disciplinary countdown and calmed himself, though he was still badly shaken. "Nightmare," he said hoarsely. "A beauty. Never had a dream with that kind of intensity before."

Rodriguez relaxed. Obviously he couldn't get very upset over a mere nightmare. "You want a pill?"

Falkirk shook his head. "I'll manage, thanks."

But the impact of the dream lingered. It was more than an hour before he got back to sleep, and then he fell into a light, restless doze, as if his mind were on guard against a return of those chilling fantasies.

Fifty minutes before his programmed wakeup time, he was

awakened by a ghastly shriek from the far side of the cabin.

Lieutenant Commander Rodriguez was having a nightmare.

When the ship made float-down on Earth a month later it was, of course, put through the usual decontamination procedures before anyone or anything aboard it was allowed out of the starport. The outer hull got squirted with sealants designed to trap and smother any microorganism that might have hitchhiked from another world; the crew men emerged through the safety pouch and went straight into a quarantine chamber without being exposed to the air; the ship's atmosphere was cycled into withdrawal chambers, where it underwent a thorough purification; and the entire interior of the vessel received a six-phase sterilization, beginning with fifteen minutes of hard vacuum and ending with an hour of neutron bombardment.

These procedures caused a certain degree of inconvenience for the Vsiir. It was already at the low end of its energy phase, due mainly to the repeated discouragements it had suffered in its attempts to communicate with the six humans. Now it was forced to adapt to a variety of unpleasant environments with no chance to rest between changes. Even the most adaptable of organisms can get tired. By the time the starport's decontamination team was ready to certify that the ship was wholly free of alien life-forms, the Vsiir was very, very tired indeed.

The oxygen-nitrogen atmosphere entered the hold once more. The Vsiir found it quite welcome, at least in contrast to all that had just been thrown at it. The hatch was open; stevedores were muscling the cargo crates into position to be floated across the field to the handling dome.

The Vsiir took advantage of this moment to extrude some legs and scramble out of the ship. It found itself on a broad concrete apron, rimmed by massive buildings. A yellow sun was shining in a blue sky; infrared was bouncing all over the place, but the Vsiir speedily made arrangements to deflect the excess. It also compensated immediately for the tinge of ugly hydrocarbons in the atmosphere, for the frightening noise level, and for the leaden feeling of homesickness that suddenly threatened its organic stability at the first sight of this unfamiliar, disheartening world. How to get home again? How to make contact, even? The Vsiir sensed nothing but closed minds—sealed like seeds in their shells. True, from time to time the minds of these humans opened, but even then, they seemed unwilling to let the Vsiir's message get through.

Perhaps it would be different here. Perhaps those six were poor communicators, for some reason, and there would be more receptive minds available in this place. Perhaps. Perhaps. Close to despair, the Vsiir hurried across the field and slipped into the first building in which it sensed open minds. There were hundreds of humans in it, occupying many levels, and the open minds were widely scattered. The Vsiir located the nearest one and, worriedly, earnestly, hopefully, touched the tip of its mind to the human's. *—Please listen. I mean no harm. Am nonhuman organism arrived on your planet through unhappy circumstances; wishing only quick going back to own world—*

The cardiac wing of Long Island Starport Hospital was on the ground floor, in the rear, where the patients could be given floater therapy without upsetting the gravitational ratios of the rest of the building. As always, the hospital was full—people were always coming in sick off starliners, and most of them were hospitalized right at the starport for their own safety—and the cardiac wing had more than its share. At the moment, it held a dozen infarcts awaiting implant, nine postimplant recupes, five coronaries in emergency stasis, three ventricle-regrowth projects, an aortal patch job, and nine or ten assorted other cases. Most of the patients were floating, to keep down the gravitational strain on their damaged tissues—all but the regrowth people, who were under full Earth-norm gravity so that their new hearts would come in with the proper resilience and toughness. The hospital had a fine reputation and one of the lowest mortality rates in the hemisphere.

Losing two patients the same morning was a shock to the entire staff.

At 0917 the monitor flashed the red light for Mrs. Maldonado, eighty-seven, postimplant, and thus far doing fine. She had developed acute endocarditis coming back from a tour of the Jupiter system; at her age, there wasn't enough vitality to sustain her through the slow business of growing a new heart with a genetic prod, but they'd given her a synthetic implant, and for two weeks it had worked quite well. Suddenly, though, the hospital's control center was getting a load of grim telemetry from Mrs. Maldonado's bed: valve action zero, blood pressure zero, respiration zero, pulse zero, everything zero, zero, zero. The EEG tape showed a violent lurch—as though she had received some abrupt and intense shock—followed by a minute or two of irregular action, followed by termination of brain activity. Long before any hospital personnel had reached her bedside, automatic revival equipment, both chemical and electrical, had gone to work on the patient, but she was beyond reach:

a massive cerebral hemorrhage, coming totally without warning, had done irreversible damage.

At 0928 came the second loss: Mr. Guinness, fifty-one, three days past surgery for a coronary embolism. The same series of events. A severe jolt to the nervous system, an immediate and fatal physiological response. Resuscitation procedures negative. No one on the staff had any plausible explanation for Mr. Guinness' death. Like Mrs. Maldonado, he had been sleeping peacefully, all vital signs good, until the moment of the fatal seizure.

"As though someone had come up and yelled *boo* in their ears," one doctor muttered, puzzling over the charts. He pointed to the wild EEG track. "Or as if they'd had unbearably vivid nightmares and couldn't take the sensory overload. But no one was making noise in the ward. And nightmares aren't contagious."

Dr. Peter Mookherji, resident in neuropathology, was beginning his morning rounds on the hospital's sixth level when the soft voice of his annunciator, taped behind his left ear, asked him to report to the quarantine building immediately. Dr. Mookherji scowled. "Can't it wait? This is my busiest time of day, and—"

"You are asked to come at once."

"Look, I've got a girl in a coma here, due for her teletherapy session in fifteen minutes, and she's counting on seeing me. I'm her only link to the world. If I'm not there when—"

"You are asked to come at once, Dr. Mookherji."

"Why do the quarantine people need a neuropathologist in such a hurry? Let me take care of the girl, at least, and in forty-five minutes they can have me."

"Dr. Mookherji—"

It didn't pay to argue with a machine. Mookherji forced his temper down. Short tempers ran in his family, along with a fondness for torrid curries and a talent for telepathy. Glowering, he grabbed a data terminal, identified himself, and told the hospital's control center to reprogram his entire morning schedule. "Build in a half-hour postponement somehow," he snapped. "I can't help it—see for yourself. I've been requisitioned by the quarantine staff."

The computer was thoughtful enough to have a roller-buggy waiting for him when he emerged from the hospital. It whisked him across the starport to the quarantine building in three minutes, but he was still angry when he got there. The scanner at the door ticked off his badge and one of the control center's innumerable voice outputs told him solemnly, "You are expected in Room 403, Dr. Mookherji."

Room 403 turned out to be a two-sector interrogation office. The rear sector of the room was part of the building's central quarantine core, and the front sector belonged to the public-access part of the building, with a thick glass wall in between. Six haggard-looking spacemen were slouched on sofas behind the wall, and three members of the starport's quarantine staff paced about in front. Mookherji's irritation ebbed when he saw that one of the quarantine men was an old medical-school friend, Lee Nakadai. The slender Japanese was a year older than Mookherji—twenty-nine to twenty-eight; they met for lunch occasionally at the starport commissary, and they had double-dated a pair of Filipino twins earlier in the year, but the pressure of work had kept them apart for months. Nakadai got down to business quickly now: "Pete, have you ever heard of an epidemic of nightmares?"

"Eh?"

Indicating the men behind the quarantine wall, Nakadai said, "These fellows came in a couple of hours ago from Norton's Star. Brought back a cargo of greenfire bark. Physically they check out to five decimal places, and I'd release them except for one funny thing. They're all in a bad state of nervous exhaustion, which they say is the result of having had practically no sleep during their whole month-long return trip. And the reason for that is that they were having nightmares—every one of them—real mind-wrecking dreams, whenever they tried to sleep. It sounded so peculiar that I thought we'd better run a neuropath checkup, in case they've picked up some kind of cerebral infection."

Mookherji frowned. "For this you got me out of my ward on emergency requisition, Lee?"

"Talk to them," Nakadai said. "Maybe it'll scare you a little."

Mookherji glanced at the spacemen. "All right," he said. "What about these nightmares?"

A tall, bony-looking officer who introduced himself as Lieutenant Falkirk said, "I was the first victim—right after float-off. I almost flipped. It was like, well, something touching my mind, filling it with weird thoughts. And everything absolutely real, while it was going on—I thought I was choking; I thought my body was changing into something alien; I felt my blood running out my pores—" Falkirk shrugged. "Like any sort of bad dream, I guess, only ten times as vivid. Fifty times. A few hours later Lieutenant Commander Rodriguez had the same kind of dream. Different images, same effect. And then, one by one, as the others took their sleep shifts, they started to wake up screaming. Two of us ended up spending three weeks on happy pills.

We're pretty stable men, Doctor—we're trained to take almost anything. But I think a civilian would have cracked up for good with dreams like those. Not so much the images as the intensity, the realness of it."

"And these dreams recurred throughout the voyage?" Mookherji asked.

"Every shift. It got so we were afraid to doze off, because we knew the devils would start crawling through our heads when we did. Or we'd put ourselves real down on sleeper tabs. And even so we'd have the dreams, with our minds doped to a level where you wouldn't imagine dreams would happen. A plague of nightmares, Doctor. An epidemic."

"When was the last episode?"

"The final sleep shift before float-down."

"You haven't gone to sleep, any of you, since leaving the ship?"

"No," Falkirk said.

One of the other spacemen said, "Maybe he didn't make it clear to you, Doctor. These were killer dreams. They were mind crackers. We were lucky to get home sane. If we did."

Mookherji drummed his fingertips together, rummaging through his experience for some parallel case. He couldn't find any. He knew of mass hallucinations, plenty of them, episodes in which whole mobs had persuaded themselves they had seen gods, demons, miracles, the dead walking, fiery symbols in the sky. But a series of hallucinations coming in sequence, shift after shift, to an entire crew of tough, pragmatic spacemen? It didn't make sense.

Nakadai said, "Pete, the men had a guess about what might have done it to them. Just a wild idea, but maybe—"

"What is it?"

Falkirk laughed uneasily. "Actually, it's pretty fantastic."

"Go ahead."

"Well, maybe something from the planet came aboard the ship with us. Something, well, telepathic. Which fiddled around with our minds, whenever we went to sleep. What we felt as nightmares was maybe this thing inside our heads."

"Possibly it rode all the way back to Earth with us," another spaceman said. "It could still be aboard the ship. Or loose in the city by now."

"The Invisible Nightmare Menace?" Mookherji said, with a faint smile. "I doubt that I can buy that."

"There *are* telepathic creatures," Falkirk pointed out.

"I know," Mookherji said sharply. "I happen to be one myself."

"I'm sorry, Doctor, if—"

"But that doesn't lead me to look for telepaths under every bush. I'm not ruling out your alien menace, mind you. But I think it's a lot more likely that you picked up some kind of inflammation of the brain out there. A virus disease, a type of encephalitis that shows itself in the form of chronic hallucinations." The spacemen looked troubled. Obviously, they would rather be victims of an unknown monster preying on them from outside than of an unknown virus lodged in their brains. Mookherji went on, "I'm not saying that's what it is, either. I'm just tossing around hypotheses. We'll know more after we've run some tests." Checking his watch, he said to Nakadai, "Lee, there's not much more I can find out right now, and I've got to get back to my patients. I want these fellows plugged in for the full series of neuropsychological checkouts. Have the outputs relayed to my office as they come in. Run the tests in staggered series and start letting the men go to sleep, two at a time, after each series—I'll send over a technician to help you rig the telemetry. I want to be notified immediately if there's any nightmare experience."

"Right."

"And get them to sign telepathy releases. I'll give them a preliminary mind-probe this evening after I've had a chance to study the clinical findings. Maintain absolute quarantine, of course. This thing might just be infectious. Play it very safe."

Nakadai nodded. Mookherji flashed a professional smile at the six somber spacemen and went out, brooding. A nightmare virus? Or a mind-meddling alien organism that no one can see? He wasn't sure which notion he liked less. Probably, though, there was some prosaic and unstartling explanation for that month of bad dreams—contaminated food supplies, or something funny in the atmosphere recycler. A simple, mundane explanation.

Probably.

The first time it happened, the Vsiir was not sure what had actually taken place. It had touched a human mind; there had been an immediate vehement reaction; the Vsiir had pulled back, alarmed by the surging fury of the response, and then, a moment later, had been unable to locate the mind at all. Possibly it was some defense mechanism, the Vsiir thought, by which the humans guarded their minds against intruders. But that seemed unlikely, since the humans' minds were quite effectively guarded most of the time anyway. Aboard the ship, whenever the Vsiir had managed to slip past the walls that shielded the minds of the crew men, it had always encountered a great deal of turbulence—plainly these humans did not enjoy mental contact with a Vsiir—but never this complete shutdown, this total cutoff of signal. Puzzled, the Vsiir tried again, reaching toward an open mind situated not far from where the one that had vanished had been. *—Kindly attention, a moment of consideration for confused other-worldly individual, victim of unhappy circumstances, who—*

Again the violent response: a sudden tremendous flare of mental energy, a churning blaze of fear and pain and shock. And again, moments later, complete silence, as though the human had retreated behind an impermeable barrier. *—Where are you? Where did you go?* The Vsiir, troubled, took the risk of creating an optical receptor that worked in the visible spectrum—and that therefore would itself be visible to humans—and surveyed the scene. It saw a human on a bed, completely surrounded by intricate machinery. Colored lights were flashing. Other humans, looking agitated, were rushing toward the bed. The human on the bed lay quite still, not even moving when a metal arm descended and jabbed a long bright needle into his chest.

Suddenly, the Vsiir understood.

The two humans must have experienced termination of existence!

Hastily, the Vsiir dissolved its visible-spectrum receptor and retreated to a sheltered corner to consider what had happened. *Datum:* Two humans had died. *Datum:* Each had undergone termination immediately after receiving a mental transmission from the Vsiir. *Problem:* Had the mental transmission brought about the termination?

The possibility that the Vsiir might have destroyed two lives was shocking and appalling, and such a chill went through its body that it shrank into a tight, hard ball, with all thought processes snarled. It needed several minutes to return to a fully-functional state. If its attempts at communicating with these humans produced such terrible effects, the Vsiir realized, then its prospects of finding help on this planet were slim. How could it dare risk trying to contact other humans, if—

A comforting thought surfaced. The Vsiir realized that it was jumping to a hasty conclusion on the basis of sketchy evidence, while overlooking some powerful arguments against that conclusion. All during the voyage to this world the Vsiir had been making contact with humans, the six crew men, and none of *them* had terminated. That was ample evidence that humans could withstand contact with a Vsiir mind. Therefore, contact alone could not have caused these two deaths.

Possibly, it was only coincidental that the Vsiir had approached two humans in succession that were on the verge of termination. Was this the place where humans were brought when their time of termination was near? Would the terminations have happened even if the Vsiir had not tried to make contact? Was the attempt at contact just enough of a drain on dwindling energies to push the two over the edge into termination? The Vsiir did not know. It was uncomfortably conscious of how many important facts it lacked. Only one thing was certain: its time was running short. If it did not find help soon, metabolic decay was going to set in, followed by metamorphic rigidity, followed by a fatal loss in adaptability, followed by . . . termination.

The Vsiir had no choice. Continuing its quest for contact with a human was its only hope of survival. Cautiously, timidly, the Vsiir again began to send out its probes, looking for a properly receptive mind. This one was walled. So was this. And all these. No entrance, no entrance! The Vsiir wondered if the barriers these humans possessed were designed merely to keep out intruding nonhuman consciousnesses, or actually shielded each human against mental contact of all kinds, including contact with other humans. If any human-to-human contact existed, the Vsiir had not been able to detect it, either in this building or aboard the spaceship.

What a strange race!

Perhaps it would be best to try a different level of this building. The Vsiir flowed easily under a closed door and up a service staircase to a higher floor. Once more it sent forth its probes. A closed mind here. And here. And here. And then a receptive one. The Vsiir prepared to send its message. For safety's sake it stepped down the power of its transmission, letting a mere wisp of thought curl forth. *—Do you hear? Stranded extraterrestrial being is calling. Seeks aid. Wishes—*

From the human came a sharp, stinging displeasure response, wordless but unmistakably hostile. The Vsiir at once withdrew. It waited, terrified, fearing that it had caused another termination. No: The human mind continued to function, although it was no longer open, but now surrounded by the sort of barrier humans normally wore. Drooping, dejected, the Vsiir crept away. Failure, again. Not even a moment of meaningful mind-to-mind contact. Was there no way to reach these people? Dismally, the Vsiir resumed its search for a receptive mind. What else could it do?

* * *

The visit to the quarantine building had taken forty minutes out of Dr. Mookherji's morning schedule. That bothered him. He couldn't blame the quarantine people for getting upset over the six spacemen's tale of chronic hallucinations, but he didn't think the situation, mysterious as it was, was grave enough to warrant calling him in on an emergency basis. Whatever was troubling the spacemen would eventually come to light; meanwhile, they were safely isolated from the rest of the starport. Nakadai should have run more tests before asking for him. And he resented having to steal time from his patients.

But as he began his belated morning rounds, Mookherji calmed himself with a deliberate effort. It wouldn't do him or his patients any good if he visited them while still loaded with tensions and irritations. He was supposed to be a healer, not a spreader of anxieties. He spent a moment going through a de-escalation routine, and by the time he entered the first patient's room—that of Satina Ransom—he was convincingly relaxed and amiable.

Satina lay on her left side, eyes closed, a slender girl of sixteen with a fragile-looking face and long, soft straw-colored hair. A spidery network of monitoring systems surrounded her. She had been unconscious for fourteen months, twelve of them here in the starport's neuropathology ward and the last six under Mookherji's care. As a holiday treat, her parents had taken her to one of the resorts on Titan during the best season for viewing Saturn's rings; with great difficulty they succeeded in booking reservations at Galileo Dome, and were there on the grim day when a violent Titanquake ruptured the dome and exposed a thousand tourists to the icy moon's poisonous methane atmosphere. Satina was one of the lucky ones: she got no more than a couple of whiffs of the stuff before a dome guide, with whom she'd been talking, managed to slap a breathing mask over her face. She survived. Her mother, father, and younger brother didn't. But she had never regained consciousness after collapsing at the moment of the disaster. Months of examination on Earth had shown that her brief methane inhalation hadn't caused any major brain damage; organically there seemed to be nothing wrong with her, but she refused to wake up. A shock reaction, Mookherji believed. She would rather go on dreaming forever than return to the living nightmare that consciousness had become. He had been able to reach her mind telepathically, but so far he had been unable to cleanse her of the trauma of that catastrophe and bring her back to the waking world.

Now he prepared to make contact. There was nothing easy or automatic about his telepathy; "reading" minds was strenuous work for him, as difficult and as taxing as running a cross-country race or memorizing a lengthy part in *Hamlet*. Despite the fears of laymen, he had no way of scanning anyone's intimate thoughts with a casual glance. To enter another mind, he had to go through an elaborate procedure of warming up and reaching out, and even so it was a slow business to tune in on somebody's "wavelength," with little coherent information coming across until the ninth or tenth attempt.

The gift had been in the Mookherji family for at least a dozen generations, helped along by shrewdly planned marriages designed to conserve the precious gene. He was more adept than any of his ancestors, yet it might take another century or two of Mookherjis to produce a really potent telepath. At least he was able to make good use of such talent for mind contact as he had. He knew that many members of his family in earlier times had been forced to hide their gift from those about them, back in India, lest they be classed with vampires and werewolves and cast out of society.

Gently he placed his dark hand on Satina's pale wrist. Physical contact was necessary to attain the mental linkage. He concentrated on reaching her. After months of tele-therapy, her mind was sensitized to his; he was able to skip the intermediate steps, and, once he was warmed up, could plunge straight into her troubled soul. His eyes were closed. He saw a swirl of pearl-gray fog before him: Satina's mind. He thrust himself into it, entering easily. Up from the depths of her spirit swam a question mark.

—*Who is it? Doctor?*

—*Me, yes. How are you today, Satina?*

—*Fine. Just fine.*

—*Been sleeping well?*

—*It's so peaceful here, Doctor.*

—*Yes. Yes, I imagine it is. But you ought to see how it is here. A wonderful summer day. The sun in the blue sky. Everything in bloom. A perfect day for swimming, eh? Wouldn't you like a swim?* He puts all the force of his concentration into images of swimming: A cold mountain stream, a deep pool at the base of a creamy waterfall, the sudden delightful shock of diving in, the crystal flow tingling against her warm skin, the laughter of her friends, the splashing, the swift powerful strokes carrying her to the far shore—

—*I'd rather stay where I am,* she tells him.

—*Maybe you'd like to go floating instead?* He summons the sensations of free flight: a floater node fastened to her belt, lifting her serenely to an altitude of a hundred feet, and off she goes, drifting over fields and valleys, her friends beside her, her body totally relaxed, weightless, soaring on the updrafts, rising until the ground is a checkerboard of brown and green, looking down on the tiny houses and the comical cars, now crossing a shimmering silvery lake, now hovering over a dark, somber forest of thick-packed spruce, now simply lying on her back, legs crossed, hands clasped behind her head, the sunlight bright on her cheeks, three hundred feet of nothingness underneath her—

But Satina doesn't take his bait. She prefers to stay where she is. The temptations of floating are not strong enough.

Mookherji does not have enough energy left to try a third attempt at luring her out of her coma. Instead, he shifts to a purely medical function and tries to probe for the source of the trauma that has cut her off from the world. The fright, no doubt, and the terrible crack in the dome, spelling the end to all security, and the sight of her parents and brother dying before her eyes, and the swampy reek of Titan's atmosphere hitting her nostrils—all of those things, no doubt. But people have rebounded from worse calamities. Why does she insist on withdrawing from life? Why not come to terms with the dreadful past, and accept existence again?

She fights him. Her defenses are fierce; she does not want him meddling with her mind. All of their sessions have ended this way: Satina clinging to her retreat; Satina blocking any shot at knocking her free of her self-imposed prison. He has gone on hoping that one day she will lower her guard. But this is not to be the day. Wearily, he pulls back from the core of her mind and talks to her on a shallower level.

—You ought to be getting back to school, Satina.

—Not yet. It's been such a short vacation!

—Do you know how long?

—About three weeks, isn't it?

—Fourteen months so far, he tells her.

—That's impossible. We just went away to Titan a little while ago—the week before Christmas, wasn't it, and—

—Satina, how old are you?

—I'll be fifteen in April.

—Wrong, he tells her. *That April's been here and gone, and so has the next one. You were sixteen two months ago. Sixteen, Satina.*

—That can't be true, Doctor. A girl's sixteenth birthday is something special, don't you know that? My parents are going to give me a big party. All my friends invited. And a nine-piece robot orchestra with synthesizers. And I know that that hasn't happened yet, so how can I be sixteen?

His reservoir of strength is almost drained. His mental signal is weak. He cannot find the energy to tell her that she is blocking reality again, that her parents are dead, that time is passing while she lies here, that it is too late for a Sweet Sixteen party.

—We'll talk about it . . . another time, Satina. I'll . . . see . . . you . . . again . . . tomorrow. . . . Tomorrow . . . morning. . . .

—Don't go so soon, Doctor! But he can no longer hold the contact, and lets it break.

Releasing her, Mookherji stood up, shaking his head. A shame, he thought. A damned shame. He went out of the room on trembling legs, and paused a moment in the hall, propping himself against a closed door and mopping his sweaty forehead. He was getting nowhere with Satina. After the initial encouraging period of contact, he had failed entirely to lessen the intensity of her coma. She had settled quite comfortably into her delusive world of withdrawal, and, telepathy or no, he could find no way to blast her loose.

He took a deep breath. Fighting back a growing mood of bleak discouragement, he went toward the next patient's room.

The operation was going smoothly. Two dozen third-year medical students occupied the observation deck of the surgical gallery on the starport hospital's third floor, studying Dr. Hammond's expert technique by direct viewing and by simultaneous microamplified relay to their individual desk screens. The patient, a brain-tumor victim in his late sixties, was visible only as a head and shoulders protruding from a life-support chamber. His scalp had been shaved; blue lines and dark red dots were painted on it to indicate the inner contours of the skull, as previously determined by short-range sonar bounces; the surgeon had finished the job of positioning the lasers that would excise the tumor. The hard part was over. Nothing remained except to bring the lasers to full power and send their fierce, precise bolts of light slicing into the patient's brain.

Cranial surgery of this kind was entirely bloodless; there was no need to cut through skin and bone to expose the tumor, for the beams of the lasers, calibrated to a millionth of an inch, would penetrate through minute openings and, playing on the tumor from different sides, would destroy the malignant growth without harming a bit of the surrounding healthy brain tissue. Planning was everything in an operation like this. Once the exact outlines of the tumor were determined, and the surgical lasers were mounted at the correct angles, any intern could finish the job.

For Dr. Hammond it was a routine procedure. He had performed a hundred operations of this kind in the past year alone. He gave the signal; the warning light glowed on the laser rack; the students in the gallery leaned forth expectantly—

And, just as the lasers' glittering fire leaped toward the operating table, the face of the anesthetized patient contorted weirdly, as though some terrifying dream had come drifting up out of the caverns of the man's drugged mind. His nostrils flared; his lips drew back; his eyes opened wide; he seemed to be trying to scream; he moved convulsively, twisting his head to one side. The lasers bit deep into the patient's left temple, far from the indicated zone of the tumor. The right side of his face began to sag, all muscles paralyzed. The medical students looked at each other in bewilderment. Dr. Hammond, stunned, retained enough presence of mind to kill the lasers with a quick swipe of his hand. Then, gripping the operating table with both hands in his agitation, he peered at the dials and meters that told him the details of the botched operation. The tumor remained intact; a vast sector of the patient's brain had been devastated.

"Impossible," Hammond muttered. What could goad a patient under anesthesia into jumping around like that? "Impossible. Impossible." He strode to the end of the table and checked the readings on the life-support chamber. The question now was not whether the brain tumor would be successfully removed; the immediate question was whether the patient was going to survive.

By four that afternoon Mookherji had finished most of his chores. He had seen every patient; he had brought his progress charts up to date; he had fed a prognosis digest to the master computer that was the starport hospital's control center; he had even found time for a gulped lunch. Ordinarily, now, he could take the next four hours off, going back to his spartan room in the residents' building at the edge of the starport complex for a nap, or dropping in at the recreation center to have a couple of rounds of floater tennis, or looking in at the latest cube show, or whatever. His next round of patient-visiting didn't begin until eight in the evening. But he couldn't relax. There was that business of the quarantined spacemen to worry about. Nakadai had been sending test outputs over since two o'clock, and now they were stacked deep in Mookherji's data terminal. Nothing had carried an *urgent* flag, so Mookherji had simply let the reports pile up; but now he felt he ought to have a look. He tapped the keys of the terminal, requesting printouts, and Nakadai's outputs began to slide from the slot.

Mookherji ruffled through the yellow sheets. Reflexes, synapse charge, degree of neural ionization, endocrine balances, visual response, respiratory and circulatory, cerebral molecular exchange, sensory percepts, EEG both enhanced and minimated. . . . No, nothing unusual here. It was plain from the tests that the six men who had been to Norton's Star were badly in need of a vacation—frayed nerves, blurred reflexes—but there was no indication of anything more seriout than chronic loss of sleep. He couldn't detect signs of brain lesions, infection, nerve damage, or other organic disabilities.

Why the nightmares, then?

He tapped out the phone number of Nakadai's office. "Quarantine," a crisp voice said almost at once, and moments later Nakadai's lean, tawny face appeared on the screen.

"Hello, Pete. I was just going to call you."

Mookherji said, "I didn't finish up until a little while ago. But I've been through the outputs you sent over. Lee, there's nothing here."

"As I thought."

"What about the men? You were supposed to call me if any of them went into nightmares."

"None of them have," Nakadai said. "Falkirk and Rodriguez have been sleeping since eleven. Like lambs. Schmidt and Carroll were allowed to conk out at half past one. Webster and Schiavone hit the cots at three. All six are still snoring away, sleeping like they haven't slept in years. I've got them loaded with equipment and everything's reading perfectly normal. You want me to shunt the data to you?"

"Why bother? If they aren't hallucinating, what'll I learn?"

"Does that mean you plan to skip the mind probes tonight?"

"I don't know," Mookherji said, shrugging. "I suspect there's no point in it, but let's leave that part open. I'll be finishing my evening rounds about eleven, and if there's some reason to get into the heads of those spacemen then, I will." He frowned. "But look—didn't they say that each one of them went into the nightmares on *every* single sleep shift?"

"Right."

"And here they are, sleeping outside the ship for the first time since the nightmares started, and none of them having any trouble at all. And no sign of possible hallucinogenic brain lesions. You know something, Lee? I'm starting to come around to a very silly hypothesis that those men proposed this morning."

"That the hallucinations were caused by some unseen alien being?" Nakadai asked.

"Something like that. Lee, what's the status of the ship they came in on?"

"It's been through all the routine purification checks, and now it's sitting in an isolation vector until we have some idea of what's going on."

"Would I be able to get aboard it?" Mookherji asked.

"I suppose so, yes, but—why?"

"On the wild shot that something external caused those nightmares, and that that something may still be aboard the ship. And perhaps a low-level telepath like myself will be able to detect its presence. Can you set up clearance fast?"

"Within ten minutes," Nakadai said. "I'll pick you up."

Nakadai came by shortly in a rollerbuggy. As they headed out toward the landing field, he handed Mookherji a crumpled space suit and told him to put it on.

"What for?"

"You may want to breathe inside the ship. Right now it's full of vacuum—we decided it wasn't safe to leave it under atmosphere. Also, it's still loaded with radiation from the decontamination process. Okay?"

Mookherji struggled into the suit.

They reached the ship: a standard interstellar null-gravity-drive job, looking small and lonely in its corner of the field. A robot cordon kept it under isolation, but, tipped off by the control center, the robots let the two doctors pass. Nakadai remained outside; Mookherji crawled into the safety pouch and, after the hatch had gone through its admission cycle, entered the ship. He moved cautiously from cabin to cabin, like a man walking in a forest that was said to have a jaguar in every tree. While looking about, he brought himself as quickly as possible up to full telepathic receptivity, and, wide open, awaited telepathic contact with anything that might be lurking in the ship.

—Go on. Do your worst.

Complete silence on all mental wavelengths. Mookherji prowled everywhere: the cargo hold, the crew cabins, the drive compartment. Everything empty, everything still. Surely he would have been able to detect the presence of a telepathic creature in here, no matter how alien; if it was capable of reaching the mind of a sleeping spaceman, it should be able to reach the mind of a waking telepath as well. After fifteen minutes he left the ship, satisfied.

"Nothing there," he told Nakadai. "We're still nowhere."

The Vsiir was growing desperate. It had been roaming this building all day. Judging by the quality of the solar radiation coming through the windows, night was beginning to fall now. And, though there were open minds on every level of the structure, the Vsiir had had no luck in making contact. At least there had been no more terminations. But it was the same story here as on the ship: Whenever the Vsiir touched a human mind, the reaction was so negative as to make communication impossible. And yet, the Vsiir went on and on and on, to mind after mind, unable to believe that this whole planet did not hold a single human to whom it could tell its story. It hoped it was not doing severe damage to these minds it was approaching; but it had its own fate to consider.

Perhaps this mind would be the one. The Vsiir started once more to tell its tale—

Half past nine at night. Dr. Peter Mookherji, eyes bloodshot, tense, hauled himself through his neuropathological responsibilities. The ward was full: a schizoid collapse, a catatonic freeze, Satina in her coma, half a dozen routine hysterias, a couple of paralysis cases, an aphasic, and plenty more—enough to keep him going for sixteen hours a day and strain his telepathic powers, not to mention his conventional medical skills, to their limits. Someday the ordeal of residency would be over; someday he'd be quit of this hospital, and would set up private practice on some sweet tropical isle, and commute to Bombay on weekends to see his family, and spend his holidays on planets of distant stars, like any prosperous medical specialist. . . . Someday. He tried to banish such lavish fantasies from his mind. If you're going to look forward to anything, he told himself, look forward to midnight. To sleep. Beautiful, beautiful sleep. And then in the morning it all begins again, Satina and the coma, the schizoid, the catatonic, the aphasic . . .

As he stepped into the hall, going from patient to patient, his annunciator said, "Dr. Mookherji, please report at once to Dr. Bailey's office."

Bailey? The head of the neuropathology department, still hitting the desk this late? What now? But of course there was no ignoring such a summons. Mookherji notified the control center that he had been called off his rounds, and made his way quickly down the corridor to the frosted-glass door marked SAMUEL F. BAILEY, M.D.

He found at least half the neuropath staff there already:

four of the other senior residents, most of the interns, even a few of the high-level doctors. Bailey, a puffy-faced, sandy-haired, fiftyish man of formidable professional standing, was thumbing a sheaf of outputs and scowling. He gave Mookherji a faint nod by way of greeting. They were not on the best of terms; Bailey, somewhat old-school in his attitudes, had not made a good adjustment to the advent of telepathy as a tool in the treatment of mental disturbance. "As I was just saying," Bailey began, "these reports have been accumulating all day, and they've all been dumped on me, God knows why. Listen: Two cardiac patients under sedation undergo sudden violent shocks, described by one doctor as sensory overloads. One reacts with cardiac arrest, the other with cerebral hemorrhage. Both die. A patient being treated for endocrine restabilization develops a runaway adrenalin flow while asleep and gets a six-month setback. A patient undergoing brain surgery starts lurching around on the operating table, despite adequate anesthesia, and gets badly carved up by the lasers. Et cetera. Serious problems like this all over the hospital today. Computer check of general EEG patterns shows that fourteen patients—other than those mentioned—have experienced exceptionally severe episodes of nightmares in the last eleven hours, nearly all of them of such impact that the patient has sustained some degree of psychic damage and often actual physiological harm. Control center reports no case histories of previous epidemics of bad dreams. No reason to suspect a widespread dietary imbalance or similar cause for the outbreak. Nevertheless, sleeping patients are continuing to suffer, and those whose condition is particularly critical may be exposed to grave risks. Effective immediately, sedation of critical patients has been interrupted where feasible, and sleep schedules of other patients have been rearranged; but this is obviously not an expedient that is going to do much good if this outbreak continues into tomorrow." Bailey paused, glanced around the room, let his gaze rest on Mookherji. "Control center has offered one hypothesis: that a psychopathic individual with stronge telepathic powers is at large in the hospital, preying on sleeping patients and transmitting images to them that take the form of horrifying nightmares. Mookherji, what do you make of that idea?"

Mookherji said, "It's perfectly feasible, I suppose, although I can't imagine why any telepath would want to go around distributing nightmares. But has control center correlated any of this with the business over at the quarantine building?"

Bailey stared at his output slips. "What business is that?"

"Six spacemen who came in early this morning, reporting that they'd all suffered chronic nightmares on their voyage homeward. Dr. Lee Nakadai's been testing them; he called me in as a consultant, but I couldn't discover anything useful. I imagine there are some late reports from Nakadai in my office, but—"

Bailey said, "Control center seems only to be concerned about events in the hospital, not in the starport complex as a whole. And if your six spacemen had their nightmares during their voyage, there's no chance that their symptoms are going to find their way onto—"

"That's just it!" Mookherji cut in. "They had their nightmares in space. But they've been asleep since morning, and Nakadai says they're resting peacefully. Meanwhile, an outbreak of hallucinations has started over here. Which means that whatever was bothering them during their voyage has somehow got loose in the hospital today—some sort of entity capable of stirring up such ghastly dreams that they bring veteran spacemen to the edge of nervous breakdowns and can seriously injure or even kill someone in poor health." He realized that Bailey was looking at him strangely, and that he wasn't the only one. In a more restrained tone, Mookherji said, "I'm sorry if this sounds fantastic to you. I've been checking it out all day, so I've had some time to get used to the concept. And things begin to fit together for me just now. I'm not saying that my idea is necessarily correct. I'm simply saying that it's a reasonable notion, that it links up with the spacemen's own idea of what was bothering them, that it corresponds to the shape of the situation—and that it deserves a decent investigation, if we're going to stop this stuff before we lose some more patients."

"All right, Doctor," Bailey said. "How do you propose to conduct the investigation?"

Mookherji was shaken by that. He had been on the go all day; he was ready to fold. Here was Bailey abruptly putting him in charge of this snark-hunt, without even asking! But he saw there was no way to refuse. He was the only telepath on the staff. And, if the supposed creature really was at large in the hospital, how could it be tracked except by a telepath?

Fighting back his fatigue, Mookherji said rigidly, "Well, I'd want a chart of all the nightmare cases, to begin with, a chart showing the location of each victim and the approximate time of onset of hallucination—"

They would be preparing for the Festival of Changing, now, the grand climax of winter. Thousands of Vsiirs in the metamorphic phase would be on their way toward the Valley of Sand, toward that great natural amphitheater where the holiest rituals were performed. By now the firstcomers would already have taken up their positions, facing the west, waiting for the sunrise. Gradually the rows would fill as Vsiirs came in from every part of the planet, until the golden valley was thick with them, Vsiirs that constantly shifted their energy levels, dimensional extensions, and inner resonances, shuttling gloriously through the final joyous moments of the season of metamorphosis, competing with one another in a gentle way to display the greatest variety of form, the most dynamic cycle of physical changes —and, when the first red rays of the sun crept past the needle, the celebrants would grow even more frenzied, dancing and leaping and transforming themselves with total abandon, purging themselves of the winter's flamboyance as the season of stability swept across the world. And finally, in the full blaze of sunlight, they would turn to one another in renewed kinship, embracing, and—

The Vsiir tried not to think about it. But it was hard to repress that sense of loss, that pang of nostalgia. The pain grew more intense with every moment. No imaginable miracle would get the Vsiir home in time for the Festival of Changing, it knew, and yet it could not really believe that such a calamity had befallen it.

Trying to touch minds with humans was useless. Perhaps if it assumed a form visible to them, and let itself be noticed, and *then* tried to open verbal communication—

But the Vsiir was so small, and these humans were so large. The dangers were great. The Vsiir, clinging to a wall and carefully keeping its wavelength well beyond the ultraviolet, weighed one risk against another, and, for the moment, did nothing.

* * *

"All right," Mookherji said foggily, a little before midnight. "I think we've got the trail clear now." He sat before a wall-sized screen on which the control center had thrown a three-dimensional schematic plan of the hospital. Bright red dots marked the place of each nightmare incident, yellow dashes the probable path of the unseen alien creature. "It came in the side way, probably, straight off the ship, and went into the cardiac wing first. Mrs. Maldonado's bed here, Mr. Guinness' over here, eh? Then it went up to the second level, coming around to the front wing and impinging on the minds of patients here and here and here, between ten and eleven in the morning. There were no reported episodes of hallucination in the next hour and ten minutes, but then came that nasty business in the third-level surgical gallery, and after that—" Mookherji's aching eyes closed a moment; it seemed to him that he could still see the red dots and yellow dashes. He forced himself to go on, tracing the rest of the intruder's route for his audience of doctors and hospital security personnel. At last he said, "That's it. I figure that the thing must be somewhere between the fifth and eighth levels by now. It's moving much more slowly than it did this morning, possibly running out of energy. What we have to do is keep the hospital's wings tightly sealed to prevent its free movement—if that can be done—and attempt to narrow down the number of places where it might be found."

One of the security men said, a little belligerently, "Doctor, just how are we supposed to find an invisible entity?"

Mookherji struggled to keep impatience out of his voice. "The visible spectrum isn't the only sort of electromagnetic energy in the universe. If this thing is alive, it's got to be radiating *somewhere* along the line. You've got a master computer with a million sensory pickups mounted all over the hospital. Can't you have the sensors scan for a point-source of infrared or ultraviolet moving through a room? Or even X rays, for God's sake: we don't know where the radiation's likely to be. Maybe it's a gamma emitter, even. Look, something wild is loose in this building, and we can't see it, but the computer can. Make it search."

Dr. Bailey said, "Perhaps the energy we ought to be trying to trace it by is, ah, telepathic energy, doctor."

Mookherji shrugged. "As far as anybody knows, telepathic impulses propagate somewhere outside the electromagnetic spectrum. But of course you're right that I might be able to pick up some kind of output, and I intend to make a floor-by-floor search as soon as this briefing session is over."

He turned toward Nakadai. "Lee, what's the word from your quarantined spacemen?"

"All six went through eight-hour sleep periods today without any sign of a nightmare episode; there was some dreaming, but all of it normal. In the past couple of hours I've had them on the phone talking with some of the patients who had the nightmares, and everybody agrees that the kind of dreams people have been having here today are the same in tone, texture, and general level of horror as the ones the men had aboard the ship. Images of bodily destruction and alien landscapes, accompanied by an overwhelming, almost intolerable, feeling of isolation, loneliness, separation from one's own kind."

"Which would fit the hypothesis of an alien being as the cause," said Martinson of the psychology staff. "If it's wandering around trying to communicate with us, trying to tell us it doesn't want to be here, say, and its communications reach human minds only in the form of frightful nightmares—"

"Why does it communicate only with sleeping people?" an intern asked.

"Perhaps those are the only ones it can reach. Maybe a mind that's awake isn't receptive," Martinson suggested.

"Seems to me," a security man said, "that we're making a whole lot of guesses based on no evidence at all. You're all sitting around talking about an invisible telepathic thing that breathes nightmares in people's ears, and it might just as easily be a virus that attacks the brain, or something in yesterday's food, or—"

Mookherji said, "The ideas you're offering now have already been examined and discarded. We're working on this line of inquiry now because it seems to hold together, fantastic though it sounds, and because it's all we have. If you'll excuse me, I'd like to start checking the building for telepathic output, now." He went out, pressing his hands to his throbbing temples.

Satina Ransom stirred, stretched, subsided. She looked up and saw the dazzling blaze of Saturn's rings overhead, glowing through the hotel's domed roof. She had never seen anything more beautiful in her life. This close to them, only about 750,000 miles out, she could clearly make out the different zones of the rings, each revolving about Saturn at its own speed, with the blackness of space visible through the open places. And Saturn itself, gleaming in the heavens, so bright, so huge—

What was that rumbling sound? Thunder? Not here, not on Titan. Again: louder. And the ground swaying. A crack in the dome! Oh, no, no, no, feel the air rushing out; look at that cold greenish mist pouring in—people falling down all over the place—what's happening, what's happening, what's happening? Saturn seems to be falling toward us. That taste in my mouth—oh—oh—oh—

Satina screamed. And screamed. And went on screaming as she slipped down into darkness, and pulled the soft blanket of unconsciousness over her, and shivered, and gave thanks for finding a safe place to hide.

Mookherji had plodded through the whole building, accompanied by three security men and a couple of interns. He had seen whole sectors of the hospital that he didn't know existed. He had toured basements and sub-basements and sub-sub-basements; he had been through laboratories and computer rooms and wards and exercise chambers. He had kept himself in a state of complete telepathic receptivity throughout the trek, but he had detected nothing, not even a flicker of mental current anywhere. Somehow that came as no surprise to him. Now, with dawn near, he wanted nothing more than sixteen hours or so of sleep. Even with nightmares. He was tired beyond all comprehension of the meaning of tiredness.

Yet something wild was loose, still, and the nightmares still were going on. Three incidents, ninety minutes apart, had occurred during the night: two patients on the fifth level and one on the sixth had awakened in states of terror. It had been possible to calm them quickly, and apparently no lasting harm had been done; but now the stranger was close to Mookherji's neuropathology ward, and he didn't like the thought of exposing a bunch of mentally unstable patients to that kind of stimulus. By this time, the control center had reprogrammed all patient-monitoring systems to watch for the early stages of nightmare—hormone changes, EEG tremors, respiration rate rise, and so forth—in the hope of awakening a victim before the full impact could be felt. Even so, Mookherji wanted to see that thing caught and out of the hospital before it got to his own people.

But how?

As he trudged back to his sixth-level office, he considered some of the ideas people had tossed around in that midnight briefing session. "Wandering around trying to communicate with us," Martinson had said. "Its communications reach human minds only in the form of frightful nightmares. Maybe a mind that's awake isn't receptive." Even the mind of a human telepath, it seemed, wasn't receptive while awake. Mookherji wondered if he should go to sleep and hope the alien would reach him, and then try to deal with it, lead it into a trap of some kind—but no. He wasn't that different from other people. If he slept, and the alien did open contact, he'd simply have a hell of a nightmare and wake up, with nothing gained. That wasn't the answer. Suppose, though, he managed to make contact with the alien through the mind of a nightmare victim—someone he could use as a kind of telepathic loudspeaker, someone who wasn't likely to wake up while the dream was going on—

Satina.

Perhaps. Perhaps. Of course, he'd have to make sure the girl was shielded from possible harm. She had enough horrors running free in her head as it was. But if he lent her his strength, drained off the poison of the nightmare, took the impact himself via their telepathic link, and was able to stand the strain and still speak to the alien mind—that might just work. Might.

He went to her room. He clasped her hand between his.

—Satina?

—Morning so soon, Doctor?

—It's still early, Satina. But things are a little unusual here today. We need your help. You don't have to if you don't want to, but I think you can be of great value to us, and maybe even to yourself. Listen to me very carefully, and think it over before you say yes or no—

God help me if I'm wrong, Mookherji thought, far below the level of telepathic transmission.

Chilled, alone, growing groggy with dismay and hopelessness, the Vsiir had made no attempts at contact for several hours now. What was the use? The results were always the same when it touched a human mind; it was exhausting itself and apparently bothering the humans, to no purpose. Now the sun had risen. The Vsiir contemplated slipping out of the building and exposing itself to the yellow solar radiation while dropping all defenses; it would be a quick death, an end to all this misery and longing. It was folly to dream of seeing the home planet again. And—

What was that?

A call. Clear, intelligible, unmistakable. *—Come to me.* An open mind somewhere on this level, speaking neither the human language nor the Vsiir language, but using the wordless, universally comprehensible communion that occurs when mind speaks directly to mind. *—Come to me. Tell me everything. How can I help you?*

In its excitement the Vsiir slid up and down the spectrum, emitting a blast of infrared, a jagged blurt of ultraviolet, a lively blaze of visible light, before getting control. Quickly, it took a fix on the direction of the call. Not far away: down this corridor, under this door, through this passage. —*Come to me.* Yes. Yes. Extending its mind-probes ahead of it, groping for contact with the beckoning mind, the Vsiir hastened forward.

Mookherji, his mind locked to Satina's, felt the sudden crashing shock of the nightmare moving in, and even at second remove the effect was stunning in its power. He perceived a clicking sensation of mind touching mind. And then, into Satina's receptive spirit, there poured—

A wall higher than Everest. Satina trying to climb it, scrambling up a smooth white face, digging fingertips into minute crevices. Slipping back one yard for every two gained. Below, a roiling pit, flames shooting up, foul gases rising, monsters with needle-sharp fangs waiting for her to fall. The wall grows taller. The air is so thin—she can barely breathe, her eyes are dimming, a greasy hand is squeezing her heart, she can feel her veins pulling free of her flesh like wires coming out of a broken plaster ceiling, and the gravitational pull is growing constantly—pain, her lungs crumbling, her face sagging hideously—a river of terror surging through her skull—

—*None of it is real, Satina. They're just illusions. None of it is really happening.*

—*Yes,* she says, *yes, I know;* but still she resonates with fright, her muscles jerking at random, her face flushed and sweating, her eyes fluttering beneath the lids. The dream continues. How much more can she stand?

—*Give it to me,* he tells her. *Give me the dream!*

She does not understand. No matter. Mookherji knows how to do it. He is so tired that fatigue is unimportant; somewhere in the realm beyond collapse he finds unexpected strength, and reaches into her numbed soul, and pulls the hallucinations forth as though they were cobwebs. They engulf him. No longer does he experience them indirectly; now all the phantoms are loose in his skull, and, even as he feels Satina relax, he braces himself against the onslaught of unreality that he has summoned into himself. And he copes. He drains the excess of irrationality out of her and winds it about his consciousness, and adapts, learning to live with the appalling flood of images. He and Satina share what is coming forth. Together they can bear the burden; he carries more of it than she does, but she does her part, and now neither of them is overwhelmed by the parade of bogeys. They can laugh at the dream monsters; they can even admire them for being so richly fantastic. That beast with a hundred heads, that bundle of living copper wires, that pit of dragons, that coiling mass of spiky teeth— Who can fear what does not exist?

Over the clatter of bizarre images, Mookherji sends a coherent thought, pushing it through Satina's mind to the alien.

—*Can you turn off the nightmares?*

—*No,* something replies. *They are in you, not in me. I only provide the liberating stimulus. You generate the images.*

—*All right. Who are you, and what do you want here?*

—*I am a Vsiir.*

—A *what?*

—*Native life-form of the planet where you collect the greenfire branches. Through my own carelessness I was transported to your planet.* Accompanying the message is an overriding impulse of sadness, a mixture of pathos, self-pity, discomfort, exhaustion. Above this the nightmares still flow, but they are insignificant now. The Vsiir says, *I wish only to be sent home. I did not want to come here.*

And this is our alien monster, Mookherji thinks? This is our fearsome nightmare-spreading beast from the stars?

—*Why do you spread hallucinations?*

—*This was not my intention. I was merely trying to make mental contact. Some defect in the human receptive system, perhaps—I do not know. I do not know. I am so tired, though. Can you help me?*

—*We'll send you home, yes,* Mookherji promises. *Where are you? Can you show yourself to me? Let me know how to find you, and I'll notify the starport authorities, and they'll arrange for your passage home on the first ship out.*

Hesitation. Silence. Contact wavers and perhaps breaks.

—*Well?* Mookherji says, after a moment. *What's happening? Where are you?*

From the Vsiir an uneasy response:

—*How can I trust you? Perhaps you merely wish to destroy me. If I reveal myself—*

Mookherji bites his lip in sudden fury. His reserve of strength is almost gone; he can barely sustain the contact at all. And if he now has to find some way of persuading a suspicious alien to surrender itself, he may run out of steam before he can settle things. The situation calls for desperate measures.

—*Listen, Vsiir. I'm not strong enough to talk much longer, and neither is this girl I'm using. I invite you into my head. I'll drop all defenses: if you can look at who I am, look hard, and decide for yourself whether or not you can trust me.*

After that it's up to you. I can help you get home, but only if you produce yourself right away.

He opens his mind wide. He stands mentally naked.

The Vsiir rushes into Mookherji's brain.

A hand touched Mookherji's shoulder. He snapped awake instantly, blinking, trying to get his bearings. Lee Nakadai stood above him. They were in— Where? Satina Ransom's room! The pale light of early morning was coming through the window; he must have dozed only a minute or so. His head was splitting.

"We've been looking all over for you, Pete," Nakadai said.

"It's all right now," Mookherji murmured. "It's all all right." He shook his head to clear it. He remembered things. Yes. On the floor, next to Satina's bed, squatted something about the size of a frog, but very different in shape, color, and texture from any frog Mookherji had ever seen. He showed it to Nakadai. "That's the Vsiir," Mookherji said. "The alien terror. Satina and I made friends with it. We talked it into showing itself. Listen, it isn't happy here, so will you get hold of a starport official fast, and explain that we've got an organism here that has to be shipped back to Norton's Star at once, and—"

Satina said, "Are you Dr. Mookherji?"

"That's right. I suppose I should have introduced myself when— *You're awake?*"

"It's morning, isn't it?" The girl sat up, grinning. "You're younger than I thought you were. And so serious looking. And I *love* that color of skin. I—"

"*You're awake?*"

"I had a bad dream," she said. "Or maybe a bad dream within a bad dream—I don't know. Whatever it was, it was pretty awful, but I felt so much better when it went away—

I just felt that if I slept any longer I was going to miss a lot of good things, that I had to get up and see what was happening in the world– Do you understand any of this, Doctor?"

Mookherji realized his knees were shaking. "Shock therapy," he muttered. "We blasted her loose from the coma—without even knowing what we were doing." He moved toward the bed. "Listen, Satina, I've been up for about a million years, and I'm ready to burn out from overload. And I've got a thousand things to talk about with you, only not now. Is that okay? Not now. I'll send Dr. Bailey in—he's my boss—and after I've had some sleep, I'll come back and we'll go over everything together, okay? Say, five, six this evening. All right?"

"Well, of course, all right," Satina said, with a twinkling smile. "If you feel you really have to run off, just when I've —sure. Go. Go. You look awfully tired, Doctor."

Mookherji blew her a kiss. Then, taking Nakadai by the elbow, he headed for the door. When he was outside he said, "Get the Vsiir over to your quarantine place pronto and try to put it in an atmosphere it finds comfortable. And arrange for its trip home. And I guess you can let your six spacemen out. I'll go talk to Bailey—and then I'm going to drop."

Nakadai nodded. "You get some rest, Pete. I'll handle things."

Mookherji shuffled slowly down the hall toward Dr. Bailey's office, thinking of the smile on Satina's face, thinking of the sad little Vsiir, thinking of nightmares—

"Pleasant dreams, Pete," Nakadai called.

Silent in Gehenna

INTRODUCTION

This is a tough story. In many ways. It deals with a subject that can draw blood—integrity, a person's honesty with himself. It's written in a style that hits hard and doesn't stop for explanations. You have to keep your eyes open and your wits sharp when you tackle this story.

This story is in the book for two main reasons. First, it's a good story. Second, it presents its own special part of the SF universe, and this book would be incomplete without a story of this type.

Harlan Ellison has been described in many ways. He's a man of strong emotions, and he evokes strong reactions in everyone who meets him—or reads his stories. One thing about Harlan: he's been there. From the troubled campuses to the back alleys of the slums, he's been there. He writes with the strength of firsthand knowledge, and with the boiling fury of a man who knows that we should be doing better than we are.

Harlan has won dozens of awards for his stories and his movie and television scripts. But his first love is SF, and he brings us here a distinctive story that tells us something important, something about ourselves.

by HARLAN ELLISON

JOE Bob Hickey had no astrological sign. Or rather more precisely, he had twelve. Every year he celebrated his birthday under a different Pisces, Gemini, or Scorpio. Joe Bob Hickey was an orphan. He was also a bastard. He had been found on the front porch of the Sedgwick County, Kansas, Foundling Home. Wrapped in a stained army blanket, he had been deserted on one of the Home's porch gliders. That was in 1992.

Years later, the matron who discovered him on the porch remarked that looking into his eyes was like staring down a hall with empty mirrors.

Joe Bob was an unruly child. In the Home he seemed to seek out trouble, in no matter what dark closet it hid, and sink his teeth into it; nor would he turn it loose, bloody and spent, till thunder crashed. Shunted from foster home to foster home, he finally took off at the age of thirteen, snarling. That was in 2005. Nobody even offered to pack him peanut butter sandwiches. But after a while he was fourteen, then sixteen, then eighteen, and by that time he had discovered what the world was really all about; he had built muscle; he had read books and tasted the rain; and on some road he had found his purpose in life, and that was all right, so he didn't have to worry about going back. And they could *jam* their peanut butter sandwiches.

Joe Bob attached the jumper cable, making certain it was circled out far enough behind and around him to permit him sufficient crawl space without snagging the bull. He pulled the heavy-wire snippers from his rucksack, cut the fence in the shape of a church window, returned the snips to the rucksack, slung it over one shoulder, and shrugged into it—once again reminding himself to figure out a new system of harness so the bullhorn and the rucksack didn't tangle.

Then, down on his gut, he pulled himself on elbows tight to his sides, through the electrified fence, onto the grounds of the University of Southern California. The lights from the guard towers never quite connected at this far corner of the quadrangle. An overlooked blind spot. But he could see the state trooper in his tower, to the left, tracking the area with the mini-radar unit. Joe Bob grinned. His bollixer was feeding back a pussycat shape.

Digging his hands into the ground, frogging his legs, flatworm fellow, he did an Australian crawl through the no-man's-land of the blind spot. Once, the trooper held in his direction, but the mini-radar picked up only feline, and as curiosity paled and vanished, he moved on. Joe Bob slicked along smoothly. (Lignum vitae, owing to the diagonal and oblique arrangement of the successive layers of its fibers, cannot be split. Not only is it an incredibly tough wood—with a specific gravity of 1.333 it sinks in water—but, containing in its pores 26% of resin, it is lustrous and self-oiling. For this reason it was used as bearings in the engines of early oceangoing steamships.) Joe Bob as lignum vitae. Slicking along oilily through the dark.

The Earth Sciences Building—Esso Hall, intaglioed on a lintel—loomed up out of the light fog that wisped through the quadrangle, close to the ground. Joe Bob worked toward it, idly sucking at a cavity in a molar where a bit of stolen/fried/enjoyed chicken meat had lodged. There were trip springs irregularly spaced around the building. Belly-down, he did an elaborate flat-out slalom through them, performing a delicate calligraphy of passage. Then he was at the building, and he sat up, back to the wall, un-Velcroing the flap of a bandolier pocket.

Plastique.

Outdated, in these times of sonic explosives and mist, but effective nonetheless. He planted his charges.

Then he moved on to the Tactics Building, the Bacteriophage Labs, the Central Records Computer Block, and the Armory. Charged, all.

Then he pullcrawled back to the fence, unshipped the bullhorn, settled himself low, so he made no silhouette against the yawning dawn just tingeing itself lightly in the east, and tripped the charges.

The labs went up first, throwing walls and ceilings skyward in a series of explosions that ranged through the spectrum from blue to red and back again. Then the Computer Block shrieked and died, fizzing and sparking like a dust circuit killing negative particles; then, together, the Earth Sciences and Tactics buildings thundered like saurians and fell in on themselves, spuming dust and lath and plaster and extruded wall dividers and shards of melting metal. And, at last, the Armory, in a series of moist poundings that locked one after the other in a stately, yet irregular rhythm. And one enormous Olympian bang that blew the Armory to pieces filling the night with the starburst trails of tracer lightning.

It was all burning, small explosions continuing to fire-cracker amid the rising sound of students and faculty and troops scurrying through the debacle. It was all burning, as Joe Bob turned the gain full on the bull and put it to his mouth and began shouting his message.

"You call this academic freedom, you bunch of earth-worms! You call electrified fences and armed guards in your classrooms the path to learning? Rise up, you toadstools! Strike a blow for freedom!"

The bollixer was buzzing, reporting touches from radar probes. It was feeding back mass shape, indistinct lumps, ground swells, anything.

Joe Bob kept shouting.

"Grab their guns away from them!" His voice boomed like the day of judgment. It climbed over the sounds of men trying to save other buildings, and it thundered against the rising dawn. "Throw the troops off campus! Jefferson said, 'People get pretty much the kind of government they de-serve!' Is *this* what you deserve?!"

The buzzing was getting louder, the pulses coming closer together. They were narrowing the field on him. Soon they would have him pinned; at least with high probability. Then the squirt squads would come looking for him.

"Off the troops!

"There's still time! As long as *one* of you isn't all the way brainwashed, there's a chance. *You are not alone!* We are a large, organized resistance movement . . . come join us . . . trash their barracks . . . bomb their armories . . . off the

Fascist varks! Freedom is now, grab it, while they're chasing their tails! Off the varks. . . ."

The squirters had been positioned in likely sectors. When the mini-radar units triangulated, found a potential lurking place and locked, they were ready. His bollixer gave out one solid buzzing pulse, and he knew they'd locked on him. He slipped the bull back on its harness and fumbled for the flap of his holster. It came away with a Velcro-fabric sound, and he wrenched the squirt gun out. The wire stock was folded across the body of the weapon, and he snapped it open, locking it in place.

Get out of here, he told himself.

Shut up, he answered. *Off the varks!*

Hey, pass on that. I don't want to get killed.

Scared, mother chicken?

Yeah I'm scared. You want to get your ass shot up, that's your *craziness, you silly wimp. But don't take* me *with you!*

The interior monologue came to an abrupt end. Off to Joe Bob's right three squirters came sliding through the crabgrass, firing as they came. It wouldn't have mattered, anyhow. Where Joe Bob went, Joe Bob went with.

The squirt charges hit the fence and popped, snicking, spattering, everywhere but the space Joe Bob had cut out in the shape of a church window. He yanked loose the jumper cable and jammed it into the rucksack, sliding backward on his stomach and firing over their heads.

I thought you were the bigger killer?

Shut up, damn you! I missed, that's all.

You missed, my tail! You just don't want to see blood.

Sliding, sliding, sculling backward, all arms and legs; and the squirts kept on coming. *We are a large, organized resistance movement,* he had bullhorned. He had lied. He was alone. He was the last. After him, there might not be another for a hundred years. Squirt charges tore raw gashes in the earth around him.

Scared! I don't want to get killed.

The chopper rose from over his sight horizon, rose straight up and came on a dead line for his position. He heard a soft, whining sound and *scared!* breezed through his mind again.

Gully. Down into it. Lying on his back, the angle of the grassy bank obscured him from the chopper, but put him blindside to the squirt squad. He breathed deeply, washed his lips with his tongue, too dry to help, and he waited.

The chopper came right over and quivered as it turned for a strafing run. He braced the squirt gun against the bank of the gully, pulled the trigger, and held it back as a solid line of charges raced up the air. He tracked ahead of the chopper, leading it. The machine moved directly into the path of fire. The first charges washed over the nose of the chopper, smearing the surface like oxidized chrome plate. Electrical storms, tiny whirlpools of energy flickered over the chopper, crazing the ports, blotting out the scene below to the pilot and his gunner. The squirt charges drank from the electrical output of the ship and drilled through the hull, struck the power source, and the chopper suddenly exploded. Gouts of twisted metal, still flickering with squirt life, rained down across the campus. The squirters went to ground, dug in, to escape the burning metal shrapnel.

With the sound of death still echoing, Joe Bob Hickey ran down the length of the gully, into the woods, and was gone.

* * *

It has been said before, and will be said again, but never as simply or humanely as Thoreau said it: "He serves the state best, who opposes the state most."

(Aluminum acetate, a chemical compound which, in the form of its natural salt, $Al(C_2H_3O_2)_3$, obtained as a white, water-soluble amorphous powder, is used chiefly in medicine as an astringent and as an antiseptic. In the form of its basic salt, obtained as a white, crystalline, water-insoluble powder, it is used chiefly in the textile industry as a waterproofing agent, as a fireproofing agent, and as a mordant. A mordant can be several things, two of the most important being an adhesive substance for binding gold or silver leaf to a surface; and an acid or other corrosive substance used in etching to eat out the lines.)

Joe Bob Hickey as aluminum acetate. Mordant. Acid etching at a corroded surface.

Deep night found him in terrible pain, far from the burning ruin of the university. Stumbling beneath the gargantuan Soleri pylons of the continental tramway—falling, striking, tumbling over and over in his stumble. Down a gravel bed into deep weeds and the smell of sour creek. Hands came to him in the dark, and turned him faceup. Light flickered and a voice said, "He's bleeding"; and another voice, cracked and husky, said, "He's siding a squirter"; and a third voice said, "Don't touch him, come on." And the first voice said again, "He's bleeding," and the light was applied to the end of a cigar stub just as it burned down. And then there was deep darkness again.

Joe Bob began to hurt. How long he had been hurting he didn't know, but he realized it had been going on for some time. Then he opened his eyes, and saw firelight dancing dimpling dimly in front of him. He was propped up against the base of a sumac tree. A hand came out of the mist that surrounded him, seemed to come right out of the fire, and a voice he had heard once before said, "Here. Take a suck on this." A plastic bottle of something hot was held to his lips, and another hand he could not see lifted his head slightly, and he drank. It was a kind of soupness that tasted of grass.

But it made him feel better.

"I used some of the shpritz from the can in your knapsack. Something got you pretty bad, fella. Right across the back. You was bleeding pretty bad. Seems to be mending okay. That shpritz."

Joe Bob went back to sleep. Easier this time.

Later, in a softer, cooler time, he woke again. The camp fire was out. He could see clearly what there was to see. Dawn was coming up. But how could that be . . . another dawn? Had he run all through the day, evading the varks sent to track him down? It had to be just that. Dawn; he had been crouched outside the fence, ready to trip the charges. He remembered that. And the explosions. And the squirt team, and the chopper, and—

He didn't want to think about things falling out of the sky, burning, sparking.

Running, a full day and night of running. There had been pain. Terrible pain. He moved his body slightly, and felt the raw throb across his back. A piece of the burning chopper must have caught him as he fled; but he had kept going. And now he was here, somewhere else. Where? Filtered light, down through cool waiting trees.

He looked around the clearing. Shapes under blankets. Half a dozen, no, seven. And the camp fire, just smoldering embers now. He lay there, unable to move, and waited for the day.

The first one to rise was an old man with a dirty stipple of beard, perhaps three-days' worth, and a poached egg for an eye. He limped over to Joe Bob—who had closed his eyes to slits—and stared at him. Then he reached down, adjusted the unraveling blanket, and turned to the cooling camp fire.

He was building up the fire for breakfast when two of the others rolled out of their wrappings. One was quite tall, wearing a hook for a hand, and the other was as old as the first man. He was naked inside his blankets, and hairless from head to foot. He was pink, very pink, and his skin was soft. He looked incongruous: the head of an old man, with the wrinkled, pink body of a week-old baby.

Of the other four, only one was normal, undamaged. Joe Bob thought that, till he realized the normal one was incapable of speech. The remaining three were a hunchback with a plastic dome on his back that flickered and contained bands of color that shifted and changed hue with his moods; a black man with squirt burns down one entire side of his face, giving him the appearance of someone standing forever half in shadow; and a woman who might have been forty or seventy, it was impossible to tell, with one-inch-wide window strips on her wrists and ankles, whose joints seemed to bend in the directions opposite normal.

As Joe Bob lay watching surreptitiously, they washed as best they could, using water from a Lister bag, avoiding the scum-coated, bubbling water of the foul creek that crawled like an enormous gray potato slug through the clearing. Then the old man with the odd eye came to him and knelt down, and pressed his palm against Joe Bob's cheek. Joe Bob opened his eyes.

"No fever. Good morning."

"Thanks," Joe Bob said. His mouth was dry.

"How about a cup of pretty good coffee with chickory?" The old man smiled. There were teeth missing.

Joe Bob nodded with difficulty. "Could you prop me up a little?"

The old man called, "Walter . . . Marty . . ." and the one who could not speak came to him, followed by the black man with the half-ivory face. They gently lifted Joe Bob into a sitting position. His back hurt terribly and every muscle in his body was stiff from having slept on the cold ground. The old man handed Joe Bob a plastic milk bottle half filled with coffee. "There's no cream or sugar, I'm sorry," he said. Joe Bob smiled thanks and drank. It was very hot, but it was good. He felt it running down inside him, thinning into his capillaries.

"Where am I? What is this place?"

"N'vada," said the woman, coming over and hunkering down. She was wearing plowboy overalls chopped short at the calves, held together at the shoulders by pressure clips.

"Where in Nevada?" Joe Bob asked.

"Oh, about ten miles from Tonopah."

"Thanks for helping me."

"I didn't have nothin' to do with it at all. Had my way, we'd've moved on already. This close to the tramway makes me nervous."

"Why?" He looked up; the aerial tramway, the least impressive of all Paolo Soleri's arcologies, and even by that comparison breathtaking, soared away to the horizon on the sweep-shaped arms of pylons that rose an eighth of a mile above them.

"Company bulls, is why. They ride cleanup, all up'n

down this stretch. Lookin' for sabooters. Don't like the idea them thinkin' we's *that* kind."

Joe Bob felt nervous. The biggest patriots were on death row. Rape a child, murder seven women, blow the brains out of an old shopkeeper, that was acceptable; but be anti-country and the worst criminals wanted to wreck revenge. He thought of Greg, who had been beaten to death on Q's death row, waiting on appeal, by a vark killer who'd sprayed a rush-hour crowd with a squirter, attempting to escape a drugstore robbery that had gone sour. The vark killer had beaten Greg's head in with a three-legged stool from his cell. Whoever these people were, they weren't what *he* was.

"Bulls?" Joe Bob asked.

"How long you been onna dodge, boy?" asked the incredibly tall one with the hook for a hand. "Bulls. Troops. The Man."

The old man chuckled and slapped the tall one on the thigh. "Paul, he's too young to know those words. Those were our words. Now they call them . . ."

Joe Bob linked in to the hesitation. "Varks?"

"Yes, varks. Do you know where that came from?"

Joe Bob shook his head.

The old man settled down and started talking, and as if he were talking to children around a hearth, the others got comfortable and listened. "It comes from the Dutch Afrikaan for earth-pig, or aardvark. They just shortened it to vark, don't you see."

He went on talking, telling stories of days when he had been younger, of things that had happened, of their country when it had been fresher. And Joe Bob listened. How the old man had gotten his poached egg in a government medical shop, the same place Paul had gotten his metal hook, the same place Walter had lost his tongue, and Marty had been done with the acid that had turned him half-white in the face. The same sort of medical shop where they had each suffered. But they spoke of the turmoil that had ended in the land, and how it was better for everyone, even for roaming bands like theirs. And the old man called them bindlestiffs, but Joe Bob knew whatever that meant, it wasn't what *he* was. He knew one other thing: it was *not* better.

"Do you play Monopoly?" the old man asked.

The hunchback, his plastic dome flickering in pastels, scampered to a roll-up and undid thongs and pulled out a cardboard box that had been repaired many times. Then they showed Joe Bob how to play Monopoly. He lost quickly; gathering property seemed a stupid waste of time to him. He tried to speak to them about what was happening in America, about the abolition of the Pentagon Trust, about the abolishment of the Supreme Court, about the way colleges trained only for corporations or the Trust, about the central computer banks in Denver where everyone's identity and history were coded for instant arrest, if necessary. About all of it. But they knew that. They didn't think it was bad. They thought it kept the sabooters in their place so the country could be as good as it had always been.

"I have to go," Joe Bob said, finally. "Thank you for helping me." It was a standoff: hate against gratitude.

They didn't ask him to stay with them. He hadn't expected it.

He walked up the gravel bank; he stood under the long bird-shadow of the aerial tramway that hurtled from coast to coast, from Gulf to Great Lakes, and he looked up. It seemed free. But he knew it was anchored in the earth, deep in the earth, every tenth of a mile. It only *seemed* free, because Soleri had dreamed it that way. Art was not reality, it was only the appearance of reality.

He turned east. With no place to go but more of the same, he went anywhere. Till thunder crashed, in whatever dark closet.

Convocation, at the State University of New York at Buffalo, was a catered affair. Catered by varks, troops, squirters, and—Joe Bob, looking down from a roof, added—bulls. The graduating class was eggboxed, divided into groups of no more than four, in cubicles with clear plastic walls. Unobstructed view of the screens on which the President Comptroller gave his address, but no trouble for the quellers, if there was trouble. There had been rumors of unrest, and even a one-page hectographed protest sheet tacked to the bulletin boards on campus.

Joe Bob looked around with the opera glasses. He was checking the doggie guards.

Tenure and status among the faculty were indicated by the size, model, and armament of the doggie-guard robots that hovered, humming softly, just above and to the right shoulder of every administrator and professor. Joe Bob was looking for a 2013 Dictograph model with mist sprayers and squirt nozzles. Latest model . . . President Comptroller.

The latest model down there in the crowd was a 2007. That meant it was all assistant profs and teaching guides.

And *that* meant they were addressing the commencement exercises from the studio in the Ad Building. He slid back across the roof and into the gun tower. The guard was still sleeping, cocooned with spinex. He stared at the silver-webbed mummy. They would find him and spray him with dissolvent. Joe Bob had left the nose unwebbed; the guard could breathe.

Bigger killer!

Shut up.

Effective commando.

I told you to shut the hell up!

He slipped into the guard's one-piece stretchsuit, smoothed it down the arms to the wrists, stretching it to accommodate his broader shoulders. Then, carrying the harness and the rucksack, he descended the spiral staircase into the Ad Building proper. There were no varks in sight inside the building. They were all on perimeter detail; it was a high caution alert: commencement day.

He continued down through the levels to the central heating system. It was June. Hot outside. The furnaces had been damped, the air conditioners turned on to a pleasant 71° throughout the campus. He found the schematic for the ducts and traced the path to the studio with his finger. He slipped into the harness and rucksack, pried open a grille, and climbed into the system. It was a long, vertical climb through the ductwork.

Climbing—

20 do you remember the rule that was passed into law, that nothing could be discussed in open classes that did not pertain directly to the subject matter being taught that day; 19 and do you remember that modern art class in which you began asking questions about the uses of high art as vehicles for dissent and revolution; 18 and how you began questioning the professor about Picasso's "Guernica" and what fever it had taken to paint it as a statement about the horrors of war; 17 and how the professor had forgotten the rule and had recounted the story of Diego Rivera's Rocke-

feller Center fresco that had been commissioned by Nelson Rockefeller; 16 and how, when the fresco was completed, Rivera had painted in Lenin prominently, and Rockefeller demanded another face be painted over it, and Rivera had refused; 15 and how Rockefeller had had the fresco destroyed; 14 and within ten minutes of the discussion the comptroller had had the professor arrested; 13 and do you remember the day the Pentagon Trust contributed the money to build the new stadium in exchange for the Games Theory department being converted to Tactics, and they renamed the building Neumann Hall; 12 and do you remember when you registered for classes and they ran you through Central and found all the affiliations and made you sign the loyalty oath for students; 11 and the afternoon they raided the basement; 10 and caught you and Greg and Terry and Katherine; 9 and they wouldn't give you a chance to get out, and they filled the basement with mist; 8 and they shot Terry through the mouth and Katherine; 7 and Katherine; 6 and Katherine; 5 and she died folded up like a child on the sofa; 4 and they came in and shot holes in the door from the inside so it looked like you'd been firing back at them; 3 and they took you and Greg into custody; 2 and the boot and the manacles and the confessions and you escaped and ran; 1—

Climbing—

Looking out through the interstices of the grille. The studio. Wasn't it fine. Cameras, sets, all of them—fat and powdered and happy. The doggies turning, turning above their shoulders in the air turning and turning.

Now we find out just how tough you really are.

Don't start with me!

You've got to actually kill someone now.

I know what I've got to do.

Let's see how your peace talk sits with butchering someone—

Damn you!

—in cold blood, isn't that what they call it?

I can do it.

Sure you can. You make me sick.

I can: I can do it. I have to do it.

So do.

The studio was crowded with administrative officials, with technicians, with guards and troops, with mufti-laden military personnel looking over the graduating class for likely impressed men. And in the campus brig, seventy feet beneath the Armory, eleven students crouched in maximum security monkey cages: unable to stand, unable to sit, built so a man could only crouch, spines bowed like bushmen in an outback.

With the doggies scanning, turning, and observing, ready to fire, it was impossible to grab the President Comptroller. But there was a way to confound the robot guards. Wendell had found the way at Dartmouth, but he'd died for the knowledge. But there *was* a way.

If a man does the dying for you.

A vark. If a vark dies.

They die the same.

He ignored the conversation. It led nowhere; it never led anywhere but the same place. The squirt gun was in his hands. He lay flat, spread his legs, feet turned out, and braced the wire stock against the hollow of his right shoulder. In the moment of light focused in the scope, he saw what would happen in the next seconds. He would squirt the guard standing beside the cameraman with the arriflex. The guard would fall and the doggies would be alerted. They would begin scanning, and in that moment he would squirt one of them. It would short and begin spraying. The other doggies would home in, begin firing among themselves, and in the ensuing confusion he would kick out the grille, drop down, and capture the comptroller. If he was lucky. And if he was further lucky, he would get away with him. Further, and he would use him as ransom for the eleven.

Lucky! You'll die.

So I'll die. They die, I die. Both ways, I'm tired.

All your words, all your fine noble words.

He remembered all the things he had said through the bull horn. They seemed far long lost and gone now. It was time for final moments. His finger tightened on the trigger.

The moment of light lengthened.

The light grew stronger.

He could not see the studio. The glare of the golden light blotted out everything. He blinked, came out from behind the squirt gun and realized the golden light was there with him, inside the duct, surrounding him, heating him, glowing and growing. He tried to breathe and found he could not. His head began to throb, the pressure building in his temples. He had a fleeting thought—it was one of the doggies: he'd been sniffed out and this was some new kind of mist, or a heat ray, or something new he hadn't known about. Then everything blurred out in a burst of golden brightness, brighter than anything he had ever seen. Even lying on his back as a child, in a field of winter wheat, staring up with wide eyes at the sun, seeing how long he could endure. Why was it he had wanted to endure pain, to show whom? Even brighter than that.

Who am I and where am I going?

Who he was: uncounted billions of atoms, pulled apart and whirled away from there, down a golden tunnel bored in saffron space and ocher time.

Where he was going:

Joe Bob Hickey awoke, and the first sensation of many that cascaded in on him was one of swaying—on a tideless tide, in air, perhaps water, swinging, back and forth, a pendulum movement that made him feel nauseous. Golden light filtered in behind his closed lids. And sounds, high musical sounds that seemed to cut off before he had heard them fully to the last vibrating tremolo. He opened his eyes and he was lying on his back, on a soft surface that conformed to the shape of his body. He turned his head and saw the bullhorn and rucksack lying nearby. The squirt gun was gone. Then he turned his head back, and looked straight up. He had seen bars. Golden bars reaching in arcs toward a joining overhead. A cathedral effect, above him.

Slowly, he got to his knees, rolling tides of nausea moving in him. They *were* bars.

He stood up and felt the swaying more distinctly. He took three steps and found himself at the edge of the soft place. Set flush into the floor, it was a gray-toned surface, a huge circular shape. He stepped off, onto the solid floor of the . . . of the cage.

It *was* a cage.

He walked to the bars and looked out.

Fifty feet below was a street—a golden street on which great bulb-bodied creatures moved, driving before them smaller periwinkle-blue humans, whipping them to push and pull the sitting carts on which the golden bulb creatures rode. He stood watching for a long time.

Then Joe Bob Hickey went back to the circular mattress and lay down. He closed his eyes, and tried to sleep.

In the days that followed, he was fed well, and learned that the weather was controlled. If it rained, an energy bubble—he didn't understand, but it was invisible—would cover his cage. The heat was never too great, nor was he ever cold in the night. His clothes were taken away and brought back very quickly . . . changed. After that, they were always fresh and clean.

He was someplace else. They let him know that much. The golden bulb creatures were the ruling class, and the smaller blue people-sorts were their workers. He was very someplace else.

Joe Bob Hickey watched the streets from his great swaying cage, suspended fifty feet above the moving streets. In his cage, he could see it all. He could see the golden bulb rulers as they drove the pitiful blue servants, and he never saw the face of one of the smaller folk, for their eyes were constantly turned toward their feet.

He had no idea why he was there.

And he was certain he would stay there forever.

Whatever purpose they had borne in mind, to pluck him away from his time and place, they felt no need to impart to him. He was a thing in a cage, swinging free, in prison, high above a golden street.

Soon after he realized this was where he would spend the remainder of his life, he was bathed in a deep yellow light. It washed over him and warmed him, and he fell asleep for a while. When he awoke, he felt better than he had in years. The sharp pains the shrapnel wound had given him regularly, had ceased. The wound had healed over completely. Though he ate the strange, simple foods he found in his cage, he never felt the need to urinate or void his bowels. He lived quietly, wanting for nothing, because he wanted nothing.

Get up, for God's sake. Look at yourself.

I'm just fine. I'm tired, let me alone.

He stood and walked to the bars. Down in the street, a golden bulb creature's rolling cart had stopped, almost directly under the cage. He watched as the blue people fell in the traces, and he watched as the golden bulb thing beat them. For the first time, somehow, he saw it, as he had seen things before he had been brought to this place. He felt anger at the injustice of it; he felt the blood hammering in his neck; he began screaming. The golden creature did not stop. Joe Bob looked for something to hurl. He grabbed the bullhorn and turned it on and began screaming, cursing, threatening the monster with the whip. The creature looked up and its many silver eyes fastened on Joe Bob Hickey. *Tyrant, killer, filth!* he screamed.

He could not stop. He screamed all the things he had screamed for years. And the creature stopped whipping the little blue people, and they slowly got to their feet and pulled the cart away, the creature following. When they were well away, the creature rolled once more onto the platform of the cart, and whipped them away.

"Rise up, you toadstools! Strike a blow for freedom!"

He screamed all that day, the bullhorn throwing his voice away to shatter against the sides of the windowless golden buildings.

"Grab their whips away from them! Is *this* what you deserve? There's still time! As long as *one* of you isn't all the way beaten, there's a chance. *You are not alone!* We are a large, organized resistance movement. . . ."

They aren't listening.

They'll hear.

Never. They don't care.

Yes! Yes, they do. Look! See?

And he was right. Down in the street, carts were pulling up, and as they came within the sounds of his voice, the golden bulb creatures began wailing in terrible strident bug voices, and they beat themselves with the whips . . . and the carts started up again, pulled away . . . and the creatures beat their blue servants out of sight.

In front of him, they wailed and beat themselves, trying to atone for their cruelty. Beyond him, they resumed their lives.

It did not take him long to understand.

I'm their conscience.

You were the last they could find, and they took you, and now you hang up here and pillory them and they beat their breasts and wail mea culpa, mea maxima culpa, and they purge themselves; then they go on as before.

Ineffectual.

Totem.

Clown, I'm a clown.

But they had selected well. He could do no other.

As he had always been a silent voice, screaming words that needed to be screamed, but never heard, so he was still a silent voice. Day after day they came below him, and wailed their guilt; and having done it, were free to go on.

The deep yellow light, do you know what it did to you?

Yes.

Do you know how long you'll live, how long you'll tell them what filth they are, how long you'll sway here in this cage?

Yes.

But you'll still do it.

Yes.

Why? Do you like being pointless?

It isn't pointless.

Why not, you said it was. Why?

Because if I do it forever, maybe at the end of forever, they'll let me die.

(The Black-headed Gonolek is the most predatory of the African bush shrikes. Ornithologically, the vanga shrikes occupy somewhat the same position among the passerines that the hawks and owls do among the nonpasserines. Because they impale their prey on thorns, they have earned the ruthless name "butcherbird." Like many predators, shrikes often kill more than they can eat; and when opportunity presents itself, they seem to kill for the joy of killing.)

All was golden light and awareness.

(It is not uncommon to find a thorn tree or barbed-wire fence decorated with a dozen or more grasshoppers, locusts, mice, or small birds. That the shrike establish such larders in times of plenty against future need has been questioned. They often fail to return, and the carcasses shrivel or rot.)

Joe Bob Hickey, prey of his world, impaled on a thorn of light by the shrike, and brother to the shrike himself.

(Most bush shrikes have loud, melodious voices and reveal their presence by distinctive calls.)

He turned back to the street, putting the bullhorn to his mouth and, alone as always, he screamed, "Jefferson said—"

From the golden street came the sounds of insect wailing.